Law of the gun

Plainsman Series

Book 1

Simon Fairfax

Corinium Associates Ltd

Law of the gun

Published by Corinium Associates Ltd.

A CIP catalogue of this book is available from the British Library

Copyright Front cover images:

More Visual Ltd

ISBN: 978-1-7391470-4-4

Info@simonfairfax.com

www.simonfairfax.com

Also by Simon Fairfax

Chapter One

The war had been over for months now and the air no longer echoed with the sound of gunfire or the raging cannons that pounded the landscape and everything before them.

The lone rider headed across the southern plains with the sun in his face. He swore he could still hear the cries of the dying in his ears and wondered how long it would be before he slept a dreamless sleep that wasn't interrupted by nightmares of the hell on earth that had been the Civil War. Despite the lessons he'd learned in the service he slouched in the saddle and took off his Jefferson Davis campaign hat every now and then to wipe his brow. The grey of his faded uniform was stained with sweat at the armpits and down his back.

He considered himself lucky that he had only had to endure one year of the horror. At seventeen he had run away from his parents' home to join up and fight for the Confederacy. Many of his older friends on the neighboring plantations had done the same thing, and he was inspired by a sense of duty and a strong desire to fight for the South and the way of life he had always known. To him it had been a thing of glory, fighting for a cause dear to the heart of every southerner he knew. Not for slavery, which many supported, because his father had no slaves upon his land and all who came to his door found refuge and salvation within. Indeed, he had befriended some of them while he was growing up and known them as companions in all manner of children's scrapes as he ran feral since moving from England as a ten-year-old. It was the proposed cession of the Southern States from the Union that was the cause to which he was drawn. This, he knew from his father and the discourse of friends, was much more complicated than a simple matter of slavery, and for him and many like him the real reason for the war was to rally under the Stars and Bars of the South for glory and honor. These valiant thoughts had soon been dispelled as the harsh realities of the war became apparent.

He rode across the gentle plains, heading toward his home in South Carolina. The horse beneath him moved easily, swishing at the long, yellowed grass, walking through the sunbaked air of the arid prairies that was hot enough to steal the breath away.

Clumps of sassafras lined the trail, giving off a wonderful fragrance that reminded him of his childhood, and drifts of willows lined the small ponds and streams that wriggled their way across the land. Occasionally he came across a buffalo wallow dug long ago by the shaggy beasts that now roamed further north and west, the earthy concave still exposed to the sky, where wild cattle now continued to roll and dust themselves in the red soil.

There were hundreds of wild steers roaming in small herds, grazing as they went, with no brands upon their hides. They cast wary glances in the rider's direction, swaying their huge spreads of horns as if to warn him off.

Suddenly the buckskin beneath him quivered slightly and the horse's ears pricked, for he knew that sound from battles past. Soon the rider too caught the sporadic crackle of gunfire. He pulled his hat tighter down on his head and pushed the buckskin into a fast canter, ever wary of gopher holes as he branched out across the grassland in the direction of the shots.

As he drew closer other sounds reached his ears, war cries and whoops. He saw in the distance an Indian running, tomahawk raised, charging towards an unseen enemy. A puff of smoke rose upwards, and the sound of a rifle shot followed quickly behind, echoing across the land. The brave looked like he'd been punched by an invisible fist as he came to a violent halt, thrown backwards by the force of the bullet hitting him in the chest, his war cry suddenly silenced.

The rider pulled out his .52 Spencer carbine from the sheath that was tied to his saddle and grasping it by the stock handle he guided his horse by leg pressure alone and levered a cartridge into the breech, cocking the hammer in a movement that spoke of long practice. He brought the rifle up to his shoulder in a single fluid movement, seeking a target as he closed upon the scene before him, still some six hundred yards away. He closed the distance fast, seeing a white man stand and turn as he was rushed from behind. The figure ignored the long gun in his left hand as his right dropped to his waist returning with a handgun that spat flame, dropping the knife-wielding Indian as he charged in for the kill.

Now less than four hundred yards away, the rider's rifle cracked, spinning another brave around. It was a lucky shot, he knew, and probably not a kill, but it would be enough to dissuade the Indian from throwing his tomahawk. He had aimed for the stomach and hit the shoulder. Cantering onwards, the gap narrowed to less than three hundred yards. Better odds. The rider worked the lever, cocked the hammer and sought his next target.

A brave had bent his bow, ready to lose an arrow, and the horseman fired again, now from less than two hundred yards, this time bringing him down with a kill. The bowman's head exploded as the lead ball hit him in the face. He knew to aim low and had judged his shot well.

The rider was now near to the last stand of the lone man, and saw that he was in a buffalo wallow, his horse on its side in the base of the hollow, either dead or well trained, its head lying on the grass as the man leant against it and used it as extra cover.

Suddenly the grass erupted in front of him as two more Indians surged upwards, cleverly concealed with seemingly no cover. Both had knives ready, held downwards, Indian style as they launched themselves from both left and right at the oncoming rider. The buckskin didn't flinch, but responded to the rider's leg pressure, slamming his chest into the oncoming red man, hooves flying as he went. The second brave grabbed the buckskin's mane with his left hand, his right knife arm stabbing down.

With no time to aim or fire the rider used the Spencer as a club, knocking the brave flying with a broken jaw, then he was through, sliding between them into the hollow as the horse locked up his haunches. Bringing himself to a halt in a shower of small stones and dust, the newcomer slid from the saddle to drop low seeking cover, the Spencer still in his hand.

"Mighty pleased to see you, friend. Your arrival was timely. All out of bullets for my Henry and down to just pistols."

"Glad I could drop by." The newcomer winked. "A fine day for it. How many are there still left out there?"

"With the two you hit on the way in, I make nary but two more that I've seen."

"What are they, Apaches?"

"'Paches? This far south? No, they be Cherokee. Brave with the war and all, the white men making fools of themselves fighting each other. They're bold now, they charge right in. The raiding's good and the white man's lands are easy pickings. They'll pull out soon as they find it ain't so easy. Leastways I hope so, if they've not too many of their own kind to call upon."

As he spoke he saw the two unwounded Indians jog off, carrying the two wounded braves with them. They headed to a copse of sweet gum and sycamores that grew further out on the plain near a small brook.

"Well they got water and we don't, so I hope that we put

'em off any more attacks. But you never can tell with Indians."

Both men looked outwards, wary and tense, and the newcomer levered a new shell into the breech of the Spencer as he did so, then held the carbine at his side. It was suddenly very quiet after the noise of gunfire, and the pall of black powder smoke had drifted upwards leaving a strangely peaceful air to the scene.

The long grass drifted with a gentle rustle in a light breeze. That appeared to be the only movement. Then there was a slightly different rustle to the grass and a brave rose up just feet from behind the pair, his knife raised, a manic war cry coming from lips that were drawn back in hatred.

The rider knew that he was not going to make it in time to shoot the Indian, even as he went through the motion of slapping his left hand onto the barrel to aim and shoot. The other man, hearing the noise, dropped and twisted around to the right. The newcomer did not believe his eyes when he saw what happened next. In a blur of movement, his new-found comrade flicked his right hand across his body to the short-barreled gun that was holstered at his belt, drawing it smoothly at the turn, so fast it appeared to leap into his hand from the belt holster and lining up on the center of the Cherokee. There was the sound of a small percussion weapon and the brave jerked twice, spasmodically in flight, the sound of the two shots rolling into one.

The newcomer stood transfixed; he had never seen action like it. He had heard about western gunfighters from the Southerners around the camps reciting the names of the famous sons of Texas but imagined it all to be exaggerated.

The gunman was still alert, his revolver cocked and ready should there be more. "Get ready to cover me," he said, dropping to reload.

"Sure." The newcomer cocked and levered the Spencer in readiness, all senses strained in case another attack came. He watched the gunman break the pistol, hinging the barrel upwards.

"Is that a model 2 Smith and Wesson?"

"Sure is, one of the new ones. Great belt gun, gets the job done even though it's just a .22, especially if you get enough lead in them in the right place."

He watched as the gunman ejected the spent cartridge cases. "Three? You shot him three times?" he asked amazed, he swore that he only heard two shots at most, that rolled as one thunderous report.

"Guess I did," the man replied nonchalantly. "Reckon I wanted him to stay down." He offered a humorless grin. With the gun reloaded, he snapped the barrel mechanism shut, span the cylinder and replaced the gun in the belt holster just to his left hand side. At which he took the reins, tugged gently, causing the well trained animal to rise, it lurched up, shook itself in a cloud of dust from the hollow and stood ready for its next command. The gunman patted it, holding the reins. "Good boy," he muttered, before turning to his rescuer. "I forgot my manners. Sam Kennedy," the gunman said as he offered his hand.

The rider tried to school his features. The name was legendary. Kennedy was a gunfighter who'd fought in the border wars as well as numerous gunfights. At first sight he did not look like the hired killer that his reputation painted him. He was slim and of medium height, but there was breadth to his shoulders. His tanned face was handsome but there was a wolf-like cautious look to his eyes that never rested. His clothes were western, but he wore a light cutaway jacket over a leather vest that gave access to both the Colt at his hip and the belt gun at his waist.

"Nathaniel Carlton, but everyone calls me Nate. Say, do you hail from Brownfield, Texas? There's a man down there the boys used to boast about could use a gun really well." It was as much as he could ask politely without causing offence.

Kennedy snorted, shaking his head. "I believe I am the same man your friends talked about," was all he said in response, his face downcast. "But I'm mighty obliged to you, things were about to get awful interestin'." Kennedy nodded at the faded grey calvary trousers. "You back from the war?"

"Yes, they asked me to stay on and help with the clerking on account of the fact that I can read and write. Now ... well now I just want to get back home and see my parents and try to forget about it all."

"Yep, war will take you like that, and the killing won't stop, I'm bound. The country's changed and not for the better. Glad I wasn't part of it."

"You didn't fight?"

"Nope. I don't agree with slavery, but I couldn't square away with fighting for the damn Yankees neither, so I did my bit to keep the borders safe from Greasers to the south and helped others where I could as a ranger," Kennedy finished, scuffing the toes of his worn-down boots as if to indicate that he would say no more on the subject. "Where's home at?

Sounds like the Deep South to me," he asked, his voice back to an easy southern drawl.

"And you'd be right. My family has a place near Greenville, South Carolina. I can't wait to get back there."

"Well, I don't wish to alarm you, but a lot has changed, what with the Reconstruction an' all. Your family, now, they farm or plant cotton?"

"We grow tobacco and run some cattle. Why would the Reconstruction, as you call it, affect me or my family?"

"Think on it. There ain't no slaves to run it no more, what with the harvest and suchlike. As I say, it's all changing. Your money's no good, Confederate currency's worthless and there ain't no work for anyone worth a hoot. Lot of ill feeling on both sides, millions of freed slaves runnin' all over and no law and order. Makes for a tolerable bad situation all round."

"Yes, I see. But we had no slaves, my father didn't hold with it. Sure we had blacks working on the farm, but we paid them a living wage and they were free to go any time they wanted. One of the reasons Father left England."

"England? I knew it. I knew that there was something off about your accent. It ain't pure south, but you hide it some, I'm bound. No offence meant." Sam Kennedy's smile took any sting from the words.

Nate smiled in return. "None taken. Yes, I hid it as we arrived here back in '57 when I was ten years old. Father still speaks like an English gentleman, so it's sort of stayed with me, but like you say it's better to hide it if you want to fit in."

"You must've been mighty young to fight then?"

"I was. I ran away at seventeen and saw only the last year of the war, thank God. It was enough. Never again."

"What say we move on? There's Cherokees in them trees over there and more of 'em may come, so I'd rather put some distance 'tween us and them. I'd admire for you to join me. I'm heading south myself and I've a haunch of venison on my horse. It ain't much but it'll serve."

"I should like that very much, thank you."

Chapter Two

The two men rode on for a few more miles until the evening started to draw in, when they found a rocky escarpment in the bed of the Yadkin River. An oxbow had formed and the water meandered slowly by. Tracks showed that all manner of wild animals came and watered here, from wild cats to unclaimed cattle and deer.

It was a peaceful setting after the afternoon's action, and they made camp in the lee of the sandstone, the exposed rock reflecting the heat of the day as the river burbled onwards, broken only by the occasional fish catching flies brought in by the cooler dusk. They hobbled their horses and left them to graze on the lush grass nearby. There was no shortage of firewood and the two men worked with the quiet efficiency of those who are at ease in the wild.

Sam was impressed by Nate's quiet economy of movement. Someone had taught the boy well, probably his father, and he wondered what manner of man would leave England

and uproot a young family for a questionable future in a newly independent America. But he knew such things were becoming more commonplace. Many Europeans had sought a new life in the States since its independence from British rule, with the promise of wealth and a new land in which to farm and prosper was beginning to encourage westward migration into uncharted lands.

Sam studied his new acquaintance. Tall at a little over six foot, he had a sparse frame that would fill out with good food and add muscle to the broad shoulders. He wore his tattered, faded uniform tunic over his cavalry pants and a standard issue twist draw holster with a button flap secured his pistol. The face was patrician, showing signs of good breeding, with sun-bleached hair beneath the campaign hat that hung from the storm strap at his throat. He squatted by the fire, sipping from a mug of scalding coffee.

"Well. That'll put the hair back on," Nate commented, wincing at the strength of the brew. "So did you grow up in Brownfield?"

"Yep. Pa had a store there. He was a gunsmith as well. One day some men came in, held up the store, wanting guns and such. Pa didn't agree and took them on. He was killed in the ruckus. There wasn't much law then, so I took out after them. Settled the account some."

"How old were you?"

"Fifteen, I guess."

"What, you took after two men at fifteen?"

"Three. Pa taught me how to shoot from an early age, started me off with a big old Colt Dragoon." He laughed.

"Damn near broke my thumb the first time I fired it. But I got mighty handy with it and my old rifle, before the new Henry there." He nodded at the butt of the rifle protruding from the saddle scabbard behind him. "Which is much improved on the old Volcanic. Anyways, I trailed the three of 'em halfway across Texas and found the last one trying to cheat at cards in a saloon. I cut in and dissuaded him. Damn near died that day, holster moved and was roughed up inside. But I survived." He shrugged, dismissing the affair.

Nate looked at the gun belt strapped at Sam's waist. It looked different to those he had seen before, then he realized why. It was the holster. "Your rig looks different. Some of the Texas boys refused the normal cavalry issue and kept their own gun belts."

"So you fought with the Texas boys? What regiment?"

"It all got a bit confused. I was mustered to one then another but ended up in the Hanover Light Dragoons under the 4th Virginia Cavalry. By the end everything was raggedy and with most of our numbers gone, why everyone was assigned every which way. Ended up in Shenandoah Valley, bloody work there." His mind drifted for a while as he remembered the horrors of those last days of the war. "Anyway, you were telling me about your gun rig," Nate answered, wanting to change the subject.

"Yep, well as I went to draw, the holster moved with the Colt, slowed me down some. It was a normal loop holster. So I got to thinking how it could be made more secure and designed my own rig. I went to a good man, a leather worker, with my ideas and he liked them and made me this. See the belt is carved longer where the holster sits. The holster loops directly through it, so when it's tied to my leg by a pigging thong it doesn't move when I draw. It's set on a back piece of leather and the lower settin' allows the belt to sit on my hip, with the holster lower to my grip. Shaved a mite off my draw time."

"You have a hammer loop though, like the others?"

"Yep, I don't want it jumpin' out and it's much better than that useless flap you have over your pistol. Prob'ly put there to stop boys shootin' their manhoods off. By the time you've unbuttoned it, twisted your hand and held the holster with the other, why the show will all be over."

Nate smiled wryly. "They say speed's fine, but accuracy's final."

"They do, and they're right, but you need both." Sam laughed.

"Will you show me? My father said you should always learn from the best. He's a great shot and he can split a wafer at twenty paces. But a speedy draw is not his forte. Father taught me how to shoot straight and hit my mark though," Nate said, and Sam detected a note of pride in the younger man's voice.

"Be pleased to. Nate, you sure do have a way with you, I ain't talked so much in a coon's age. But before we do anythin', you need to get rid of that useless rig that you have there. Ain't no good to man nor beast. But maybe we'll practice some on the trail and see how you can shoot once the gun is out.

"Next decent town we find, we'll see if they have a good saddler and get you fixed up. They'll be glad of the work and no mistake. What are you packing there, a Colt?"

"Yes, a Navy .36." Nate unbuttoned the flap and withdrew the gun, handing it to Sam.

Sam accepted the revolver, liking the balance, pinwheeling it upon his trigger finger as it flashed in the firelight and the dying rays of the sun. "Nice balance, six chambers loaded?"

Nate was puzzled. "Yes, why not? They're there, so I use them."

"Some gunmen keep the chamber under the hammer empty to prevent a misfire and blowin' their foot off – or worse, like I said earlier." Sam offered a wry grin. "Me, well like you, I'm of a mind to keep her fully loaded, because if you need that extra bullet it's no time to be struggling with re-loading. Nice gun, anyways." He spun it, did a reverse Road Agent's Spin and handed the pistol butt first to Nate.

"How did you do that?"

"I'll show you some time, but we'll do the basics before we get onto the tricks. Get the gun out smoothly, choose your target and squeeze the trigger. Speed will come with practice."

"But why the second gun?" Nate was intelligent and had an enquiring mind. He was fascinated by this new skill and keen to learn as much as he could.

"I use a Colt Army in my right holster. Long barrel as you know, so it's difficult to draw when you're in the saddle. This way..." His hand flew across in a blur of movement and the Smith & Wesson appeared magically in his hand. "...I can draw really quickly while I'm on horseback. Also, it gives me extra firepower if I need it. Gotta be careful, mind, the barrel's shorter and there's a tendency to sweep too far across on the crossdraw to get an instinctive alignment."

"Yeah, I understand," Nate said.

"Here endeth the first lesson." Sam smiled.

Chapter Three

The next day Sam and Nate continued traveling through the plains of the southern states, heading due south until they came to Salisbury. It was a decent sized town lying by the banks of the Yadkin River, and Nate remembered it from his younger days. They halted a little way out of town, their caution born of war or potential enemies making them keen to understand how the land lay before moving into a new situation.

"Used to be a pretty little town," Nate said. "It sets well by the river there and the parks are mighty green. I hope it hasn't changed much. I had heard that there was a large prison camp here that was relieved by a raid in April. It decimated the town they say, so there might be a lot of bad feeling. I've had enough of trouble, so I hope it's settled down now."

"We'll see soon enough, but keep your Spencer handy. Nothing like a rifle at close quarters for dissuading folks from causing trouble," Sam remarked sardonically.

They walked their horses into the town from the north, kicking up whorls of dust from the dry and hardpacked street. The town looked run down and shabby, with recent evidence of burned out buildings and a few boarded up stores. A Stars and Stripes flag flapped in the faint breeze above a command post with two soldiers standing at attention outside dressed in Union blue uniforms. The soldiers gave the newcomers a hard stare, noting the campaign hat and grey Confederate trousers Nate was wearing. The two men ignored the stares. They passed down the main street and asked a passer-by if there was a livery stable in town. With directions secured they entered and paid for a couple of stalls and began unsaddling their horses.

The old ostler, like most of his breed, was talkative and as nosy as western etiquette would allow. He took his pipe from his mouth and asked: "Come far?"

"Yep, from up north, near the Appomattox," Nate replied.

"You there at the surrender?"

"I'm afraid I was, but I'm glad that it's all over."

"Shameful thing that, never thought I see or hear of the day. General Lee alright? I'd heard he warn't very well?"

"The general? Yes, he's fine," Nate said. "Don't believe all you hear. Sad and worn out, but fine. Now you're a local man, which is the best saloon where a man could get a beer?"

"Was I you, I'd try the Double Dice. She's quiet and you don't get many bluebellies in there. But have a care, son, they still don't cotton to those wearin' the grey. Was I you, I'd shift myself out of those togs if you want a peaceful life."

Nate looked down at his travel worn trousers and

shrugged. "Obliged for the advice, friend. I guess a beer and a bath, and some new clothes wouldn't go amiss."

"Have one for me. I may be over later when I get finished up here."

The two men hoisted their saddles onto the wooden burrow, removed their rifles and walked stiff legged in the manner of horsemen towards the Double Dice. The batwing doors swung open as Nate pushed inwards, shoving his hat back on the storm string as he did so.

Sam was more wary, stepping inside and moving away to the left, so as not to be outlined and allowing his eyes time to adjust to the relative gloom of the bar.

Nate reached the bar and looked back, surprised at his newfound friend's actions. He shrugged and ordered. "Two cold beers, barkeep, and best be ready for two more to follow, it's been a long ride on a hot day."

The barman, a jovial looking man with a white apron around his upper body, smiled at Nate's words and produced two frothing glasses that he set down on the counter. Nate saw Sam walk across the room in the mirror behind the bar. It was just after twelve and the saloon was half full.

"That'll be two bits, but I gotta tell you, American money only. We don't take no Confederate currency in this town no more."

"That's alright, I've few Yankee dollars here." With which Nate slapped a dollar on the bar top.

The two men drank deeply, each draining half the glass in one swoop.

"Yankee dollars, the man says. Did you listen to him,

Perry? Anyone would think he won the war, being a Johnny Reb an' all."

Nate caught the reflection in the mirror. The speaker was a broad sergeant, sitting with two non-coms at a nearby table. Nate ignored him and took another pull at his beer, smacking his lips.

"He ignored you, sarge. Guess it's that yellow stripe running down his leg, must go right through I guess." One of the two soldiers sneered. "That'll be why the Rebs wear grey. It's better to hide the yellow than good old blue. Whaddya say, Johnny Reb?" he taunted.

Nate looked around, noting the hard look that had been coming into Sam's eyes. He was almost unrecognizable as the easy going companion from the trail that they had shared together. Nate swallowed his anger and his pride, turning with a false smile. "Sergeant, the war is over, why don't we let it be, huh?" he said, turning back to his beer.

"Yep, like all them Johnny Rebs, yeller through and through."

Nate looked at Sam, whose eyes were slits of evil. He'd had enough. "Well if your mouth was the size of a regiment of cavalry, why you'd have won the whole damn war in about two days, all the noise you create," Nate said.

The bar erupted into laughter. The sergeant pushed back his chair, knocking it over as he reached for the flap of his campaign holster. At the action, Nate picked up his Spencer and cocked the hammer, pointing the large caliber weapon at the belly of the loudmouthed sergeant.

"No gunfights in here, gents, take her outside if you want to shoot each other," the barman called, producing a sawn-off shotgun from under the bar and waving it menacingly at both parties.

The sergeant laughed. "Why I ain't gonna pull a gun. I just aim to pin back his ears and swallow him whole."

The other two soldiers laughed at this. The sergeant had been the victor of many a barroom brawl and held his stripes largely on account of the fact that he could lick any man in his platoon and keep them in good order for the officers. At six foot with a board stretch to his shoulders, Muldoon had a deep chest and presented an imposing figure. His nose was pushed to the side from a previous break, and the scar tissue around his eyes hinted at a fighter's background. His belly protruded, but the fat hid a slab of hard muscle. He advanced, his lumpen fists raised. "Don't you worry, barkeep, I'll pay for the damage. It'll be a pleasure to wipe the floor with this Johnny Reb. I'll win the war again all on my ownsome, so I will. Come on, sonny, hit me if you can," he jeered.

Nate pushed his rifle back to Sam, slid off his hat and raised his fists.

Sam muttered, "You sure about this? You're takin' in a wide belt of country there. Me, I'd as soon shoot the bastard."

"Well if he starts to stomp my head, then you can shoot him with my blessing," Nate muttered. He turned and walked straight into a roundhouse punch from the sergeant. He saw stars as he barely managed to avoid the full force of the blow, which sent him staggering to the bar. He held on, shook his head and dodged a driving knee that was aimed at his groin, spinning along the bar and staying upright.

"Come back and fight, yeller boy!" Muldoon ordered with a sneer.

Nate raised his hands in a boxer's stance, moving them slowly in time, now both ready and wary. He feinted with his leading left, got inside the sergeant's guard and hooked a massive right to the man's hard belly. A brief exhale of breath was his only reward as Sergeant Muldoon kept coming in, and two brawny arms encircled him, starting to squeeze. Nate felt himself lifted from his feet, ribs in agony as the pressure increased.

Wise to the ways of roughhouse brawling, Muldoon dropped his head forward to prevent a Liverpool kiss.

As the agony knifed through him, Nate saw his chance and bit down hard on one of the protruding cauliflower ears. Muldoon howled in agony, raising his head up and sideways, and Nate drove his forehead down, smashing into the bridge of his nose, crushing the cartilage to pulp. The grip broken, Nate moved backwards, heaving in deep breaths. Both men circled now, wary, and Muldoon moved in his ham-like fists, circling, throwing a left then a right-left combination.

Nate blocked the first two, but the third punch caught him on the side of his ear, sending stars flashing in front of his eyes. Muldoon moved in close, keen to get at him and Nate threw him with a rolling hip lock and staggered back to get his wind and balance.

Muldoon bounced onto the wooden floor and staggered upright. "Oh, you've done it now, lad. I'm gonna kill you." He snarled and waded in, arms bent and raised, leaving his hard belly unguarded but protecting all his upper body and head. Nate looked quickly behind and seemed to dance back and away, looking for space between the scattered tables.

"Stand and fight, yeller boy!" Muldoon strode forward seeking to close again.

Then it happened, and those that saw it were not sure that they registered the move properly. Muldoon was out of punching range and Nate stepped back on his left foot tilting his upper body back at almost forty five degrees. His right leg shot up, bent at the knee, snapping straight at the last minute and driving the side of his foot straight through Muldoon's guard as the bootheel smashed into his chin, forcing the shattered jaw backwards, unhinging it to hang loosely. Muldoon cried out in agony before crashing backwards to smack his head upon the floor, out cold. Nate pulled back his leg in perfect balance, stepping lightly into a fighting stance in case Muldoon somehow managed to get up.

The bar was in awed silence, having seen but not really believed what had occurred. The two enlisted men started to grab for their pistols from the clumsy flapped holsters, then froze.

Sam Kennedy produced his Colt with a flash of speed and had it lined up on both men, hammer back, before either of them had the chance to even reach their weapons. "You just sit tight, gents, and keep your lives. The boy won fair and square. So why don't you just pick up that dumb ox and drag him off to the surgeon. If he's lucky his big mouth might work again someday."

The two soldiers looked at each other and went to pick

up the recumbent form of the sergeant, still not believing what they had witnessed.

Once they had gone, Sam holstered the Colt. "Nate, I do declare you are a wonder. I thought he had you backing up for sure and I was all set to shoot him in his darn-fool head. What just happened?"

Nate grinned, rubbing his head, and before he could answer the barman shouted. "Drinks on the house, boys. Son, you deserve more than a beer. Have a whiskey on me and I'd admire to know your name. That goddamn loud-mouth Yankee's had it comin' since the day he first set foot in here." He offered Nate his hand.

"Nathaniel Carlton, but I go by Nate. How do you do?"

"Here's to you, sir." Sam and the barkeep raised their glasses, saluting Nate.

"Now tell me all. How'd you learn to fight like that?"

"My father used to spar with his friends at a boxing gym in London. He even managed a few rounds with the great Tom Sawers, though he could never lay a glove on him unless he allowed him to, so he says. Well, he taught me how to box and it was bellows to mend at first. I'd come in from the yard with a black eye and my mother would give him what for, I can tell you. Then I improved and in the end I could hold my own."

"But that kick. I ain't never seen nothing like it," the barkeep said.

"We had a French Creole cook came up from New Orleans. By the good Lord could she cook. I tell you, I have missed her cooking," Nate mused, licking his lips. "Anyway, her husband was a French Savate fighter called Michel

Casseux. He was a champion from New Orleans and he taught me as well. A bit of dirty fighting too, but all's fair in love and war." Nate grinned. "Comes in handy against a bigger opponent when he's not expecting it."

"Well you sure gave that Yankee a good hiding," Sam said. "But now I reckon we should make ourselves scarce just in case those soldier boys get frisky and come back here lookin' for trouble."

They went to the store where Nate bought some new clothes, a black low-crowned J. B. Stetson and a pair of chaps. "I don't know what's been happening at home, but the thought of getting all torn up if I go brush popping after strays does not appeal. Do we look for a saddler here too?"

"No, let's get ourselves a little closer to your home. If he's any good it'll take a few days and you don't want to be hanging around here near the fort, because as sure as eggs are eggs them soldiers will be back and they'll lengthen the odds some, you can count on it."

After a trip to the bathhouse and the local eating house, the two men moved onto the road again. When they stopped for the night Sam gestured to his gun. "Forget getting the pistol out fast, let's see how you shoot. No speed, mind, just show me if you can shoot straight."

Sam set six fir cones up on a log about twenty five yards away. He stepped to the side. "Okay, let's see how you do. Nice and steady."

Nate drew his Colt, eased back the hammer, aimed and squeezed the trigger. The first cone shattered as the bullet hit it. Five more times he caught the hammer on the recoil and each time a cone disintegrated. Smiling, he began to reload the pistol.

"That's some good shooting. Your father taught you well and you can sure see straight. We'll make a pistolero of you yet. But now we have to make sure its instinctive alignment and you ain't just sighting down the barrel."

Chapter Four

They reached Charlotte by the late afternoon of the next day and booked into one of the hotels on Tryon Street. Despite the war and the battles that had been fought here the town seemed less down at heel than Salisbury. The cotton mill was still working, and groups of former slaves now labored as they had before to unload the huge bales and push them onto the docks from the wagons.

There were bullet holes in some of the buildings, but the townsfolk weren't wary of the two strangers as they rode down the street and the atmosphere was not as strained as it had been further north. Nate put some of it down to the fact that he wasn't wearing Confederate colors anymore. With the horses stabled and rooms booked they went in search of a saddler.

In the store they looked over the display of bridles, saddles, and all manner of leather goods. There was a glass display case with a handful of guns for sale laid out on green baize. The glass was polished, and the guns were free of dust. Sam noted this and thought that it boded well.

"Can I help you gents?" the man behind the counter asked. He was lean of build and friendly in his manner. He had the thick fingers and large knuckles of a man who worked with leather. It spoke well of him as a tradesman in Sam's eyes.

"I sure hope so," Sam replied. "We're after something special in the way of a holster for a belt gun. Do you carve your own work or buy it in?"

The man snorted in disgust. "The only thing I buy in is the leather and I oversee how that is tanned and treated my own self. If you want something in leather I can make it. I have all sorts to suit the item you require. I don't come cheap, I'll warn you, but you'll get the quality you're after, of that I'm sure. Name's Thomas Tilbury, and I'm the third generation of leather workers since my grandpa apprenticed in London sixty years ago. Now what can I do for you?"

Both men took to the owner, who was clearly proud of his work.

"I'm Sam Kennedy, this is Nate Carlton. We'd admire to see if you can make something like this," he offered, pointing at his gun belt and holster.

"Sure. Take it off and let me have a better look." Sam did so reluctantly, he instinctively hated others touching his guns or gun belt.

Tilbury handled Sam's belt and guns with reverence and care, as if he was used to people reacting the way Sam did. "Nice work," he commented. "Very nice indeed. Sam

Kennedy, you say? You happen to hail from southwest Texas?"

Sam nodded, immediately wary.

"Thought so, seems I might have heard of you. You as good as they say you are?" he asked looking over horn-rimmed spectacles that were perched on his nose.

"Ain't no one killed me yet," Sam replied.

"I gotta say I like the fixed loop arrangement and the lowered lip of the belt. Who's it for? 'Cause I like to see it fitted and up against my customer's hip. There ain't two hips the same." The two men liked the leather man more as he talked.

"It's for Nate here, to replace that useless bucket he has riding on his hip at the moment," Sam joked.

Nate raised his eyebrows and shook his head.

"What you got in there now?"

Nate pulled open the holster and slid out the pistol. "Colt Navy .36."

"May I?" Tilbury took the weapon. "Nice gun. Little small in caliber but she'll do the job, no doubt about it. And do you want a belt holster like this fella too?"

"No, sir, just the one will do."

"Very well." Tilbury took Sam's rig to the counter and produced a pencil and a large sheet of paper. Setting the gun belt and holster out flat, he drew around the outline and proceeded to measure Nate for his hips and arm length.

"You two fellas gone be around for a day or so?" They nodded. "Good. I'll cut out a rough pattern for the belt and the backing leather. I've got an old Navy in the back I'll use as a template and put it all together roughly at first and see how she sits on you. Come in tomorrow and we'll see how we get on. I've got some nice supple leather – strong mind – that'll do well."

They promised to return and went out and around the town getting their bearings. The local hide and tallow factory on the outskirts of town appeared to be doing good business and smelled as bad as such factories always did. Cattle moved listlessly around the holding pens as if they were resigned to their fate.

"Such a shame," Nate commented. "Wasting all that meat, I mean. Bodies just get dumped in the river when the hide's off 'em. People starving everywhere and no food in places, especially up north. There's no beef up there. A crying shame."

"They say the railroad's been cut at Columbia and there ain't no stock cars, anyways. How you gonna get enough cows up there to make it worthwhile? And who's gonna pay for it? Maybe one day they will when they fix the goddamn railroad, but now? No sirree," Sam said.

"Drive 'em?" Nate suggested.

"From this far southeast? Sure they done some over to Texas up through the Shawnee trail, but from here? Naw. An idea though from Texas, mebbe."

They bought a couple of cold beers in the cool of the bar and were immediately approached by two of the girls. They were pretty and friendly, just the way they were paid to be. Susie paired up with Nate, flirted with him and asked him to buy her a drink. It was the same old game, but both men had been short of female company for so long that they were more than happy to pay for the entertainment.

Nate had had enough by late evening and headed back toward the hotel. Sam stayed on for a game of poker. The stakes were low, but he enjoyed the game for its own sake, and with a girl on his arm he was relaxed and happy. An old riverboat hand had taught him how to play most of the variations of the game, and he'd learned all the tricks: stacking, bottom dealing, how to build a deck, slipping, negating the cut. But he never cheated in a straight game; he was good enough not to need to.

The day ended with Sam the better off by a good few dollars, and the next morning they went back to see Tilbury who, good as his word, had the first model for the gun belt and holster ready for them. It was carved in the bright orange leather of new hide but would need a little trimming and stitching after final corrections for the fit.

Nate strapped the thick gun belt about his lean waist, buckling it and pushing his Colt into the empty holster, checking the way it felt. Tilbury clearly had a good eye. It sat neatly upon his hips and felt comfortable. A length of pigging thong hung from the bottom to secure the lower end of the holster to his thigh.

"Just tie her off and we'll see how she feels," Tilbury said. "Nothing completely fixed yet, so we can adjust it any way you want. Now how's that?"

"Feels good. Might be a tad too far back from my hipbone, but apart from that it's perfect," Nate replied.

Tilbury came in and made a few final adjustment markings where he would need to trim and alter the leather. "Good. Now, I'll oil up the old Navy model I have in the back and soak the leather in a clean bowl of water for a few hours, so that when it dries it'll fit the contours of the gun. Like I say, it's gonna shrink a mite."

Nate was pleased with the result, marveling at how different it felt to the ungainly military belt he'd worn for the past year or so.

Chapter Five

Two days later Nate was getting itchy feet. He was keen to be off back home. After being soaked, the leather had dried well in the heat and he was now the proud owner of a new gun belt and holster. After Tilbury oiled it, the leather was much darker and duller than before and a small-buckled strap around the holster added to the flair of the design. It was a little touch Tilbury had added and it meant that Nate could tighten the grip a little if he had to as the leather wore in. He bought more boxes of cartridges, powder and ball from Tilbury and percussion caps to practice, and Sam was going to show him how to draw and fire from the hip from what he hoped would one day be a faster draw than his old cavalry rig.

At first Nate felt self-conscious about carrying such an ostentatious display of firepower, but as they rode the trail he got more used to it. They stopped early some thirty miles south of Charlotte, where the cottonwoods offered good shade by a stream that ran through small lakes and water-holes. They made camp for the night by one of the lakes as the cicadas and crickets started chirping.

Every time they had stopped for water or a rest that day, Sam had shouted "draw!", and each time Nate had thought, reacted and started to cock the weapon as he pulled the gun from his new holster. He began slowly and on Sam's instruction he'd removed a cartridge from the chamber under the hammer. Twice the hammer had slipped when he tried to cock it too fast and hit down on the percussion cap guarding the empty chamber. Each time Nate cursed his lack of skill.

"It'll come," Sam said. "Relax. Smooth first, speed later. We know that you can shoot at targets with the gun out, we just need to put the two together." Sam encouraged Nate and showed him again the action of raising the thumb to engage with the hammer and pull back smoothly as the gun came level clear of the holster before pulling the trigger. "It'll take time. Your muscles have to remember so it becomes second nature. The speed will come, trust me. Now, an hour a day on static practice will build up your mind and your muscles so it becomes the most natural thing in the world."

And so they continued, and to reciprocate Nate helped Sam with two books that he had with him, going through Charles Dickens' *Oliver Twist* and helping him with the words that he was unfamiliar with.

"Now this is the stuff of real learnin'," Sam declared. "Why the language is so special. This is more valuable than anything I'm teaching you."

"Everything has its value, Sam, each to its own time and place. But with an education a man can really make something of himself, at least that's what my father told me.

These will be interesting years ahead, a new time in this great nation, with opportunities abounding, I'll wager."

"Well, I'd like to share your optimism, Nate, I surely would. But I think there'll be more pain before we see the right of it, you mark my words," Sam replied.

The training continued, and by the time they came to Greenville three days later, Nate found that the movement was becoming smooth. He was still slow compared to Sam, but the draw was becoming much more fluid and natural.

They walked their horses slowly down the main drive from the trail to the plantation where Nate had spent most of his formative years. He smelled the familiar odor of tobacco plants that had grown well as workers walked the lines picking the huge leaves. He didn't recognize any of the workers, so he rode on up to the house.

Large cottonwoods and shady lime trees lined the drive and opened out into a wide arching rotunda that would allow carriages to pull up and circle before being driven off. Nate was puzzled. The grass was unkept and weeds now dotted the gravel of the drive. The whole scene looked shabby and untidy.

But Sam was impressed. He whistled and said: "Is all this yours?"

He saw before him a large white clapperboard house on three stories with a red tiled roof. The porch to the front shaded a large veranda, and circular columns gave a distinctive colonial feel to the property. The windows were of multipaned design with drapes hanging at each side. There was a feeling of opulence about the whole place that was difficult to define. A stable block lay off to the right, and further away tobacco sheds and store houses were a bustle of activity.

The heat was stifling, Nate removed his hat to wipe his sweat-streaked forehead. "My mama will not be pleased to see me returning in such a state of disarray," he commented.

"I doubt she'll care too much. She'll just be pleased to see you home safe, I'd wonder."

Both men dismounted, but Nate was puzzled that no one had come out to take their horses. He moved off around to the stables at the side of the house and found them fouled and empty and sour with the smell of stale feed. The two men tied their horses to a rail inside a large barn partitioned for stalls.

"You alright? You look kinda worried," Sam asked him.

"Something doesn't feel right. Someone should have been down to look to the horses, and everywhere's a mess."

"Maybe things have changed. Maybe there ain't no servants or staff to spare after the war an' all." Sam shrugged, but he bent in the time honored fashioned to tie the pigging thong to his leg and ease off the toggle holding his Colt in place.

Nate was not quite as practiced yet, and thought he would not need his gun, not here of all places. Some of the workers looked up as they strolled to the main steps of the house, then looked away, avoiding their eyes. Nate removed his hat and struck it against his chaps and shirt, raising dust in a small cloud. They came to the front door and Nate turned the handle, nervous somehow at returning after so long away. He had not told his parents when he left, as he knew they would try to stop him. Instead he had left them a letter explaining his actions.

"Hello? Father, Mama? Is anyone home?" he called out. A figure appeared, a black girl, dressed in a mop cap and flannel dress.

"Can I he'p you, sir?" she asked hesitantly, holding her hand to partially hide her face. A purpling bruise was evident against the skin on her cheekbone and she looked like she'd been crying.

"Yes, you certainly can. I am Nathaniel Carlton. This is my house – or rather my father's. Where are my parents?"

"Sir, you be the son of Master Charles?" Her eyes widened in fear.

"I am. Where are they?"

Sam noticed that Nate's voice had become haughtier and more authoritative, and his British accent more pronounced.

The girl turned without a word and ran back along the hall to the door on the left from where she had emerged, a room Nate remembered as his father's study. Nate and Sam heard voices and then a slap of a hand on skin and a cry of pain. The two men looked at each other as a figure left the room. It was not the girl but a white man, tall and ill-kempt, hair shiny with bay rum, a once white shirt open almost to the navel and some sort of uniform trousers held up by suspenders. There was an arrogance to his walk and in one hand he carried a brandy glass, swilling the amber liquid within it.

"Well, well. The prodigal returns. I do declare you've changed a bit, Naathaneeeale." The man deliberately drew out the name. He was clearly drunk, or partly so, as his face had a sheen of sweat induced by more than just the humidity. Nate noticed that he had a small caliber pistol shoved into belt.

"Craw Gillett! What the hell are you doing in my parents' house?" Nate did not raise his voice, yet the anger was palpable.

"Ha! Ain't that just so typical of you Carltons? Well, I got news for you, boy, it ain't your parents' house nor even yours no more. Do you know what?" Here he paused as two more figures shadowed out of the study. They were both unshaven and stank of sweat and booze even from this distance. They were rough looking, and one of them had left his trousers unbuttoned. They came forward to flank Gillett. "Boys, this here is that Johnny Reb son of a bitch I was telling you about. As big a traitor as his father."

The two men at his side offered Nate and Sam evil grins through yellow teeth. One of them had a Remington in his belt, the other carried a quirt.

"Get out of my house, you bastard, and take these two with you. Where are my parents?"

Gillett sneered. "They're dead, boy. Dead and buried as the traitors they were. This house, now, she belongs to me and you're trespassing. Now you get out before I shoot you, too." Gillett's had dropped to the pistol at his waist. "And take your swish with you," he ordered, nodding at Sam and failing to notice just how dangerous he was.

Nate was but three feet from Gillett, smelling the stale body odor and the cigars and liquor on his breath. The punch when he swung his fist was a good one. It came from nowhere and landed solidly on Gillett's jaw, knocking him over to land him on his back on the hardwood floor with a crash. The brandy glass smashed by his side, spraying glass fragments and brandy across the dusty floorboards. Gillett rubbed the blood from his lips, his face contorted in anger, and went to pull the gun from his waist. One of the two men at his side went to pull the Remington and the other raised the quirt to strike.

All three halted mid action. Sam had drawn his Colt in a blur of motion, hammer eared back to cover all three men faster than they would have believed possible. There was no drama, just a wicked smile as if Sam were begging the men to carry on doing what they'd been threatening to do. They knew then that they had underestimated him. A townsman, they'd thought, seeing his neat jacket and polished boots, all dressed up in a gun rig trying to look tough.

"Now gents, you just take those pistols out between two fingers. You try anything with me and I'll blow your damn heads off and sleep all the easier for it. And you, mister, drop that quirt 'cause I'd like nothing better than to shoot your arm all bloody, especially if you been usin' it on that poor girl in there." The quirt was dropped and the guns gingerly removed and placed on the floor next to the whip.

Nate was hyperventilating at Sam's side, having failed to pull his gun out because he had left the hammer loop in place.

"You shoot me, you bastard, and you're as good as dead." Gillett snarled. "I'm a captain in the state police and you'll be hung before midnight. The governor's in charge and there'll be a wanted poster with your name on it, dead or alive. We rule this state now, soldier boy. Not you, Reb scum. So back off. This ain't your house or your land no more. It was forfeited and now belongs to the State, and that means me." Gillett stood, suddenly empowered by the silence and feeling safer now that he had declared his position. He wiped a trickle of blood from his chin and bent to pick up his pistol.

"I'd leave that alone if I were you," Sam said. "I'd as soon shoot you as not, police or no. 'Cause if you'n are all dead, who's gonna say who killed you?" He gave wicked smile. "Now kick them pistols over here. Nate, don't you go off half-cocked on me and shoot this bastard, much as you might want to. Let's hear what he has to say."

Nate had gone white, and unshed tears glistening in his eyes. His voice was raw with emotion when he spoke: "Who killed my father and why?"

Gillett hesitated, a sure sign that he was lying. "I ain't exactly sure, but he was accused of aiding the British to break the blockade with arms and provisions out of Charleston. He denied it and was shot in the kerfuffle." Gillett shrugged.

"And my mother?"

"Way I heard it she got caught in the crossfire," Gillett finished lamely.

"You weren't there?"

"Nope. Well, I was in the yard, but it was dark and who knows who shot who or where. Anyways, this house and the land that goes with it were sequestered, signed by a judge and the governor. So you can go whistle, Dixie." Gillett sneered once more, feeling braver as each minute passed. At his words, steps were heard from outside and shadows fell across the main doorway.

Sam did a Border Shift from right to left and pulled his

Smith and Wesson, now covering both the door and the three men. Nate slipped off the loop and drew his own Colt, cocking the hammer in readiness. Two more rough-looking men appeared at the door in state police uniforms, holding rifles at the ready.

"What's going on here?" the one with a sergeant's stripes on his arm demanded.

"I'm sure glad you boys arrived when you did," Gillett drawled. "These men were just fixing to rob us. Looks like a stalemate to me, Nate."

"Might be a stalemate from where you're standing," Sam said. "But me I know you're going to be waiting in Hell when I slide on down there. Nate here doesn't give a damn, you just told him you murdered his family. So call her anyway you want, because my thumb is getting plum tired holding back this hammer."

Gillett looked at Sam, a nervous tic forming in his eye. He saw indecision written on the sergeant's face. "Okay, so what do you want, Nathaniel?"

"I want some personal effects of my parents and some things from my room. Let me get my carpet bag and I'll be gone. Then I'll be back to do it legally and see you hung for the murdering bastard that you are."

Sam held them back, continuing to line on Gillett as Nate passed behind him without blocking his field of fire.

He ran up the stairs to his old room at the back of the house. Pushing open the door he saw it was a mess, with an unkept bed, clothes everywhere and drawers pulled out onto the floor. He shook his head in disgust and sadness. This was his home, and now it was defiled, and his parents gone, the suddenness of it all still not registering with him properly. He grabbed his old carpet bag that lay on the floor near a cupboard and put in a broken photo of his parents and some personal effects from his childhood. He took one last look at the room and walked calmly out and back down the stairs, holding back his anger and his tears.

Chapter Six

The scene at the bottom of the stairs had changed little in his absence. Sam's guns were still drawn and focused, the new arrivals still held their rifles and Gillett was still cursing. To Nate's eyes it looked like a Mexican stand-off.

"Now, you've got what you came for, get the hell out," Gillett said.

"One more thing. Where is Patch?"

"What, that damned Paloosy stallion? Him and me have had words and he's none the better for it. Goddamn horse nigh on killed me."

"What did you do to him? Did you kill him, too?" Nate snapped.

"No, he's in the lower corral. But you won't get anywhere, he's wild and he's only good for dog meat. Anyway's he's mine, belongs to the estate."

Before anyone could move, Nate drew his Colt and placed it right under Gillett's jaw, earing back the hammer.

"No he is not. I bred him from a stallion that father traded from the Nez Perce. He's mine and I'm taking him."

The beads of sweat that reappeared on Gillett's forehead had nothing to do with drink.

"Take the damned hellion, then. See if I care."

Nate nodded and started to walk backwards, once again making sure that he didn't block Sam's line of fire.

"Anyone comes out that door in the next few minutes I'll shoot first and ask questions later," Sam said. "Nate, cover me with your Spencer, then we get the horse."

"Sure thing, Sam." Nate raised his rifle and covered the men as he and Sam backed carefully toward the front door.

"Who are you, mister, another Johnny Reb?" Gillett smirked at Sam.

"Nope. I didn't fight in the war. Sam Kennedy's the name."

"*Kennedy*! The Brownfield gunman?" Gillett gasped, realizing how close he had come to death.

Normally Sam was reticent about his growing reputation, but sometimes he knew it helped avoid trouble. "The same. Now I'd admire for you gents to just back off while I leave your company," Sam said with a tight-lipped and humorless smile.

He edged carefully through the doorway and walked crabwise down the steps, his eyes steady on the group of men. Nate turned and ran for the barn, where he quickly saddled the two horses. Sam raised his gun one final time and Gillett and his companions flinched and took a few steps back into the house. Sam backed slowly toward the barn, his eyes on the door and the windows facing out from the house, guns at the ready. Nate had brought the horses to the barn door and they both mounted and were just about to ride off when they heard a noise. A rake fell with a clatter and there was the sound of a woman's sob. A face appeared from around the stall. It was Millie, the maid who had let them in. Her dress was torn and she held it to her breast to preserve her decency with one hand, tears running down her bruised face.

"You alright, girl? What happened?" Sam asked, although it was pretty evident to both men's eyes.

"Them men in the house, Gillett and his friends, they did this to me. I 'scaped through the French windows while you were holdin' them off in the hall. Take me with you, sir, please. just as far as town if'n that's where you're goin'. Please, sir, I swear I'll be no bother," she pleaded.

"Can you ride, girl?" Sam asked, at which she nodded. "Hop on behind me while we go get Nate's horse."

Sam slipped a foot from his stirrup and pulled the girl up behind him. She clung around his waist, holding on for grim death, and the two shot out of the back door of the barn toward the far corral. They skidded to a halt and Nate cursed as he saw the state of the Appaloosa that stood trembling before him. The horse's eyes were wild, and he was starey-coated and thin, with ribs showing beneath the mangy skin. He was unshod and his hooves were chipped. There were quirt marks on his haunches across the black and white blanket spot. The stallion shook his head up and down, his eyes wild with fear and distrust.

Nate slipped off the buckskin and went for a halter hanging on the corral post as Sam turned and watched the track that led back to the house, his hand over his hip and Millie still holding on behind him. Standing before Nate was what had once been a magnificent quarter horse cross blanket spot Appaloosa stallion. As he approached the horse it rolled its eyes and laid its ears back. Nate approached steadily but smoothly, head held low, shoulders relaxed, talking softly in terms that were meaningless to human ears. The flared nostrils breathed in his scent, once, twice, and then the horse snorted, pawing the ground with his hoof. Nate stopped and breathed steadily, knowing every breath and beat of his heart could be heard by the horse. Looking up from beneath his hat he saw the marks of a ghost cord about the lower jaw and cursed inwardly, struggling to keep his anger, his demeanor and therefore his heartbeat low.

Finally, the ears came forward as Nate moved into that magic spot within the horse's area of trust. He finally secured a position beneath the throat lash and put his arms gently around the strong neck. The horse, to his relief, remembered him.

"Easy boy, easy," he muttered and gently brought the halter to bear, strapping it about his head. Turning to the side he beckoned to the horse gently. The animal resisted at first, then reluctantly followed him to the lowered corral rails. With steady movements he approached his buckskin and mounted, leading the Appaloosa by the halter rope. Sam took a final look back toward the house and nodded, and they moved off slowly at first and then sped up into a steady ground-eating lope, putting distance between themselves and Nate's childhood home.

They made it to the town of Greenville later that afternoon and went straight to the livery stable. Once inside Nate saw to his buckskin and then proceeded to care for the stallion, gently washing him off with a damp sponge and warm water. Having fed and watered him, he let him be to enjoy the fresh hay in his stall.

"That damn Gillett needs a damn good whipping for what he did to that horse. I should like to teach him the error of his ways someday. Now, Millie, do you know anyone in town that you can stay with? Is Ma Bertha's restaurant still renting rooms?"

"She is, sir, but I don' know she'll allow me in what with one thing and another." She looked embarrassed. "But sir, I do know Moon. He's sort of a relative. He's here in town they do say as how he done left the planation when your mammy and pappy was killed."

"Moon? He's here in town? Well I'll be. I thought he was pretty much part of the furniture back home. Let's get you to a doctor and have you taken care of, and I'll go find Moon while you're there."

They found a doctor, and leaving Millie with him the two men went off to track down Moon. The doctor told them he was working for the local blacksmith, who wasn't hard to find. They heard the steady ring and fall of a hammer across two streets and found him on the outskirts of town.

The blacksmith's premises comprised a two-story building with a large lean to off the side of the street, housing the forge and offering space to shoe horses and fashion steel.

Banging away with a hammer was one of the biggest men Sam had ever seen. He stood about six four and must have weighed a good two hundred and fifty pounds. But none of it was fat. His arms bulged with muscles and his chest was broad and deep. He wore a scruffy undershirt beneath a suede apron and was sweating profusely as he labored, his head bent forward in concentration over his work. His dark skin was covered with a sheen of sweat that accentuated the corded rippling muscles. The movement of the strangers arriving caught his eye and he looked up to see who it was. His face broke into a surprised smile and Sam could see how he got his nickname. The face was round and gentle, shaped like a full moon. "Master Nate, I do declare, you're alive!"

"It would appear so, Moon, though everyone seems surprised."

The huge man put down the hammer and tongs, rubbed his massive hands on his apron and came over shaking Nate's hand in a vicelike grip, making him wince with the power. Nate introduced him to Sam and they briefly caught up on the time he'd been away.

"I'm surely sorry 'bout your folks. They was always good to me and the others." His face saddened as he spoke. He went on to explain how it had happened. "It was that no good Gillett. Him and some others from the state police. They turned up one night, scheming bunch, walked right in and accused your pappy of being a traitor to the Union for helpin' the British bring in supplies to the Confederacy from ships at Charleston. Mebbe there's some truth to it, I don't know, but Gillett sure as hell wanted to be the big man and take your house.

"Anyways, we heard gunfire in the yard and the upshot was your parents got shot. Guess they forced his hand, damn Carpetbaggers." He carried on explaining all that had gone on to the surprised Nate and Sam. "Seems we ain't no better off, neither. Sure we're free 'n' all, but we don't like it that the Yankees used us as an excuse to change the South with their big words. That there Gillett, now, he employs all the other slaves, pays them nothin' and takes money for keep and board, so he says." Moon spat into the dust of his yard. "He couldn't give a good goddamn, treats them worse than the slaves they was—not that they was slaves under your pappy."

Nate told him about Millie. Moon was incensed at the news, and promised he would find her work and see her right. "I tell you, master Nate, one dark night me an' Mister Gillett are goin' have words and it ain't gonna be pretty."

"You be careful, Moon. Seems to me he's got the whole area tied up and he might not be the only one. They'll find any old excuse to hang your kind, with or without a trial. The South seems to have lost the war in more ways than one. And on Gillett, you'll have to get in line, because he has it coming to him and no mistake. It's just a matter of how and when." Nate's face was a mixture of sadness and hatred for the new owner of his parents' home.

"I'll be right along to the docs. I'll just tell Mr. Morgan I'll be back shortly." He disappeared into the workroom and came back minus the apron and wearing a shirt over his huge shoulders. They walked along to the doctors and Moon swore again when he saw the state of Millie, even though she looked a lot better than she had before.

"You hold on now, girl, I'll get you a new dress. That one just ain't decent no more." The three men shook hands and left as Moon went off to the general store to buy Millie some clothes.

Later, seated in the saloon and sipping their beers, Sam opened the conversation that sat between the two men like a chasm. "Nate, I know you're hurtin' and I'm right sorry for your parents 'cause I know how it feels, but some things have to be said and at the right time." Nate looked up at Sam moodily from his beer that he had been staring at with unfocused eyes. "The thing is, Nate," Sam continued, "you've been getting better with that Colt, the drawing and the accuracy both. You've got a ways to go yet, but you're gettin' there. But it ain't enough. You damn nearly got yourself killed today because you weren't ready.

"Your instincts told you something was wrong, but you ignored them. You got to learn to trust your instincts because they'll save your life. Being fast on the draw isn't enough. Now this here is a rough country and it's getting worse, not better. There's no law to speak of and what there is, is corrupt. A man has to stick up for hisself to stay alive. That loop should have been off that hammer as soon as you stepped down off'n that horse and sensed something was wrong, you hear me?"

Nate hesitated as though he had not understood the words then slowly nodded his head in agreement. "You're right, Sam. I have a lot to learn in many ways, and I'll mind what you say and be more aware. Especially now that I'm alone. Or, as alone as I can be out here with all my family back in England.

"I also have my own score to settle, but not yet. I have to be better prepared and like I told Moon, pick my own time and place. But first I have something to do. It's not legal and it carries an element of risk. So if you want to stay out of it,

I'll understand, but I'd be obliged if you'd tell anyone who asks that I was with you all night, okay?"

"Now I know you've landed on your head and had all the sense knocked out of you. Wherever you're goin' I'm comin' along, if only to stop you getting your darn-fool head blown off. Now, what're you up to?"

So Nate told him.

Chapter Seven

They retraced their steps in the dark and arrived at the Carlton house in the early hours of the morning. They left the horses hobbled in a nearby cave that Nate had played in as a boy. It was a good spot and led onto a little known back trail that would take half the time off their journey back to Greenville. The trail was nearly overgrown, and no one seemed to have used it in a long time. The scrub and brush had pushed through the sandstone pass to the extent that if you didn't know it, you'd never find the start of the trail or the recessed cave. It brought them out about a quarter of a mile from the back of the house. Both men wore moccasins, fetched from their saddlebags.

They moved from cover to cover and finally reached the back of an old outhouse, listening for any movement or tell-tale signs that someone knew they were there. No lights showed and no noise came from anywhere. The old family dog had either died or more likely been shot, Nate thought to himself, knowing Gillett's cruelty. The bunk houses for the workers were about two hundred yards off to the west and nobody stirred from there either. Everywhere was quiet.

The air was still with a sticky heat and the sweet smell of soil baked by the hot sun. It was humid and both men were sweating.

Nate pushed his low crowned Stetson back onto its storm strap and moved off in a crouch.

Sam, his gun drawn, waited and watched, straining to hear anything untoward. Looking at the white boards of the house he spotted Nate outlined in the darkness at the French doors of his father's old study.

Nate's breathing was shallow, his nerves on edge as he too listened intently. The catch was as poor as it had always been and with the aid of his clasp knife he prized open the lock just as he had done as a child, sneaking back into the house late at night after forbidden adventures. Slipping through the open doorway he was into the familiar surroundings of the room, which was now a mess. There were papers everywhere, scattered cushions from the chairs and the smell of stale cigars, cheap perfume, and brandy. He walked carefully over to the full length wall cupboards and opened one of the bottom doors. The old books were still there, which he removed before pressing the two floor-boards. They sprang up on a secret catch and beneath was a small combination safe. Nate dialed the set combination engraved on his memory and found to his relief his father had not changed it. Feeling inside, he retrieved two bags of gold coins his father always kept there and a large bundle of US dollars in a paper band. Then his fingers found an enve-lope that he had not expected. He struggled to read the writing in the near darkness and pushed it inside the saddle-bags he had brought along. He closed the safe quickly, replaced the books and shut the cupboard door. He gave one final look around the room, knowing that it would never be the same again. So many good memories had been defiled. His eyes held the polished wooden box on one of the shelves and reaching for it he found his father's matched dueling pistols within. Taking the box carefully he made for the French doors and was about to relatch the door when he made a sudden decision. He would never be back, all that was once here was gone forever. He returned, lit an oil lamp and dropped it on the floor near the drapes. He closed the door quickly and watched as the hungry flames leapt and caught at the tinder dry wood and material. Within seconds the whole room was irredeemably ablaze. Nate and Sam ran back to cover and watched as the fire took hold.

When they were nearly back at the horses, Nate drew his pistol, fired it into the air and shouted: "Fire, fire! The house is on fire!"

Soon they saw lights ablaze at the bunkhouse and the upstairs windows of the main house. Bells rang and confusion reigned. The two men saddled up, and for a moment they remained motionless. Nate watched as his family home burned and he felt as though all ties with the past were being severed and that he was now adrift in a new, uncertain, and empty world.

They rode back to town through the shortcut. Approaching quietly through a dry wash, they picked up the Appaloosa and the rest of their bags from behind the livery stable and rode quietly out into the darkness. The riders moved all night and by morning they were well on their way to Columbia. They had ridden hard and in silence, each man keeping his own council. They made a dry camp and five days later boarded a riverboat on the Broad River that would take them on down to Columbia and Charleston.

With the horses loaded, the flat-bottomed paddle steamer huffed its way southwards, passing through a green land of lakes and streams. Small forests and tall river birch, beech and blackgum trees lined the sandy shores.

The two men leant on the rail of the upper deck watching the water and the scenery drift by before them, disturbed only by the hustle and noise aboard the vessel.

"It sure is lovely country down here," Sam said. "Different to Texas and the borders. Mind, they have a beauty of their own. Wilder, rawer, if you take my meaning."

"I can imagine. It is beautiful, but it reminds me too much of home, I need to keep moving. I'll go with you to Charleston and see the sights and the ocean, maybe send a letter home to try to find George and let him know what's happened."

"He's older than you?"

Nate nodded. "Yep, by about eight years, and he was away in the army. God knows where he is now. But we have family in London and Hertfordshire. I'll send it to the old family estate. We sold a lot of it off, but I hear there are still some holdings there."

"Sounds mighty impressive. Why did your father leave England if he was well set up there?" Their friendship had grown, and Sam felt it was no longer a prying matter.

Nate laughed harshly, more like a bark than a laugh.

"You'll never believe the irony." He paused shaking his head, still angry and upset at the death of his parents. "After the Slave Trade Abolition Act in 1807, my father became a member of the Anti-Slavery Society with Wilberforce and others. Long and short of it, there was still a lot of slaving going on illegally. Well, the story goes that he was at his club one day in London and another member was in his cups. He started an argument with him, insulting my father. It got heated and my father called him out."

"Wait, he called him out to a duel like in the stories of lords and ladies and such?" Sam asked incredulously.

Nate sighed. "Alright, I wasn't going to say anything, and gunslinger or not I will cook your wagon for you if you breathe a word to anyone." Sam promised yet felt puzzled, and Nate continued. "My father was an earl. He was Lord Sinclair-Carlton of Eastham."

Sam's face broke into a big grin, and he started to laugh.

"Sam, you promised now."

Sam struggled to contain himself and said sotto voce, "You mean all this time I've been traveling with a real honest to goodness lord? Waal, I'll be, I mean your lordship, sir."

Nate shook his head in disgust, but Sam noted that it was the first time in days that he had smiled. "Like I was saying ... they arranged the date and met. My father, as I told you, was a crack shot and had served in the army in India, and he killed his man. It was a fair fight but there was a hullabaloo and Father had to flee from prosecution. The man he killed was rich and influential. So we came here. He believed that this was his last chance and that eventually slavery would be abolished here anyway, so he did what he could to help any slave that sought sanctuary on our land.

"But he didn't like bullies, and he felt that the North was bullying the South. So, he stood up for his principles, and for that matter, so did I." The bitterness returned to Nate's voice, and he sank back into himself again. There had been a tightness about him that had been growing since leaving Greenville. He was a changed man, even more than he had been by the war.

He practiced more with the gun, drawing and shooting when he could. Sam would shout 'draw' at any given moment and instinct and second nature had taken over. He was getting faster and smoother. They walked down the deck to the rear of the boat where no one was about, with the sun starting to slip down in a spectacular blaze of orange strips shot with vermillion reaching across the sky like a flaming comet. Both men were seemingly relaxed.

"Draw!" Sam called and matched his own action with that of Nate's, pulling his pistol. Two hands moved in a blur of action, two Colts appeared as one, cocked ready and aimed at an imaginary target.

"Damn it, boy, you're getting real fast. I'd swear you nearly shaded me there," Sam offered.

Nate's response was a wan smile.

"Come on, let me buy you a drink and play a few hands of poker. See if we can't have some fun with these here riverboat gamblers."

Sam, Nate had learned, was a dab hand at cards. He could build a stacked deck, negate a cut, and he knew all manner of tricks and the dark arts of double dealing. Most of the time he played fairly, but he knew when cheating was happening, and when it did he out-cheated the cheater. The riverboats were a hard school, and all manner of men frequented the games on board, from straight players to card sharks. Sam had taught Nate some of the techniques and occasionally they sought to out-cheat each other for fun.

They entered the saloon from the deck and were met by the smell of cigar smoke and whisky. A dining area was set up at the far end of the saloon, but near the front a slatted wooden screen shielded the area of play, and two poker games were already under way. Smoke above the two tables of green baize hung in layers, penetrated only by the glow of the oil lamps on the walls and the single downlight above the table. The two moved across to the dining tables and ordered some food. Strong coffee ended the best meal that they had eaten in a while, and they went over to the card tables.

There was the same mix on the boat that could be found in pretty much any western town in this new world. A couple of cowhands lounged at the bar with the stakes too high for them, while two whisky drummers sat playing blackjack with the house dealer. The two games of poker had attracted a crowd and one was clearly running much higher stakes than the other.

A chair was free, and Sam moved to take it. Nate stayed back; he had no wish to enter such a game and preferred to watch.

"Room for a littl'un?" Sam asked gently.

A man who appeared to be a professional gambler held the deck. The frills on his shirt beneath his black jacket were white in the low light, a string tie was tied at his throat. He had quick hands with long, tapering fingers, Sam noticed. Smoke dribbled from the long cheroot in his mouth, and he squinted against it, sizing Sam up. He had no gun in evidence to both Sam and Nate's keen eyes.

"Sure, if you can make the stakes. Five card stud, table stakes only, five dollars minimum bid, no limit." The gambler raised an inquiring eyebrow.

"Sounds fine by me. Evening gents, I'm Sam."

"I'm Abe, this John, Phil and Mike," the gambler replied. The others were a mix of professional looking men along with another whiskey drummer.

The play began and was brisk with keen betting. For Sam it was one of those days when it seemed he could do no wrong, and he wondered if he was being set up for a big fall. He won two out of three pots, the money rising in front of him.

"Looks like the luck is with you, sir," the drummer called Phil remarked, but there was a taint to the comment that did not go unnoticed by Sam. It was always the same, a stranger starts winning and everyone goes sour.

"Just the luck of the cards, friend. If you want to change seats, be my guest," he offered blandly.

"No, just sayin' is all, no offence."

Sam nodded genially. The game continued and then for Sam the moment came. He was dealing, the cards were cut, and he flipped them out across the baize. His hole card was a king of hearts. The bidding went up steadily. The gambler, Abe, looked at him curiously as the ace of hearts dropped face up on the fourth card drawn. Sam knew he was pleased that he hadn't got a royal flush. The last card to fall in front of Sam was the nine of hearts. He had a straight flush. Three aces were showing on Abe's cards. It came down to Sam and the gambler as the others dropped out. There was now over a hundred and fifty dollars in the center pot and the tension was palpable. The gambler licked his lips.

"I'm calling you, mister." At which he matched the bid and flipped over the fifth card, a big grin upon his face. It was the fourth ace. Sam reckoned that the pack was light. There was just something in the feel that told him. Now he knew it. Abe had been dealing before and somehow he had held back the ace or maybe two. Sam's face showed nothing. He turned over his fifth card carefully. The nine of hearts.

"Sorry, Abe. Looks like you're outvoted. Straight flush."

The gambler's face was murderous. "Open your palms mister and drop the cards."

There was a gasp and the other players moved back. Nate had been studying the play but had kept a wary eye on the room. He saw a movement out of the corner of his eye, a jacket moved back to reveal a holstered pistol. The man looked mean, with hard, sharp eyes. He was to Sam's right and would be hard to deal with in the event of trouble.

Sam's hands were now free, his right having disappeared off the table, but his Colt was clearly still in his holster.

"You saying I'm cheatin'? Is that it? You held the aces, you thought you filled your hand the way you wanted. Apologize if you don't mean it that way and I'll just walk away. Your choice." Sam looked straight into the gambler's eyes, his voice brittle.

Abe's manner changed as the tension dropped from his shoulders. "Sorry, Sam. Why sure, I guess you're right. I'm just a bit sore at losing all that money. Hope you'll give me the chance to win it back." He finished with an insincere smile.

"Later, maybe." Sam started to push back his chair slightly as a prelude to standing.

"Waal no hard feelings," Abe drawled.

Two things happened very fast. Abe shot his right hand forward as if to shake hands with Sam, then there was a concussion of black powder as he flew backwards, collapsing into his chair, his face creased with pain. Behind Sam another gunshot sounded a fraction after his. A figure to his right collapsed, dropping a pistol from a limp right hand.

"It's alright, Sam. I had him covered." Nate's voice came across, and with it a nervousness born of his first close quarters shooting outside of the war.

"He's dead," came the voice of one of the townsmen who had attended the game as he looked at the two holes in the slumped gambler's body that had bled all over his white shirt. "And he wasn't wearing no gun, mister."

Sam had now stood up so that all could see the Smith & Wesson in his right hand.

"Check his right sleeve." Sam nodded at the dead gambler. The townsman did so and found a Derringer in a spring sleeve quick draw rig.

"Well I'll be!" he exclaimed. "How did you know?"

"Saw him favoring his right arm and carrying it a mite strangely. Laid my pistol in my lap when I could see he was gettin' agitated. Good job I did or I'd be dead now." He then turned to face his friend. "Obliged to you, Nate. I hadn't clocked him at all."

"I saw him get ready. He loosed off his hammer loop and was starting to draw. I had to step in or you'd have been shot by now. I guess they were working together, but I left it to the last second until I was certain."

"He's tellin' the truth," one of the cowhands piped up. "I saw it and was goin' for my own pistol, but damn me, you're fast, mister. I ain't never seen anything like it. You gave him every doubt before you drew."

The captain arrived, pushing through the crowd to see what had occurred. He was lean, smooth and had the weathered face of a man who'd spent many years on the river. He had a pistol in his hand at the ready. His voice when he spoke was clear and direct: "Now what in tarnation is going on here? Who started this and who did the shootin'?"

The townsman, Mike, spoke up. "'Twas a fair fight, Captain. This man here." He pointed at Sam. "Was accused of cheating by this gambler. He backed off and then Abe there pulled a hideout gun but lost out. It was fair shootin' no mistake. A second later and Sam here would've been dead."

"What about this gent?" the captain asked looking at the dead gunman on the floor, the pistol near his hand where it fell.

Nate spoke up: "He figured to backshoot Sam and I had to stop him. I gave him every chance, but he was intent on backing up the gambler and killing my friend."

The captain looked hard at both men. "It happened like they said, cap'n," offered the cowhand from the bar.

"Very well. I must say I don't like gunplay on my boat. I

can see it was a fair fight, but I'll need your names for the authorities as I shall have to report it."

"I'm Sam Kennedy, this is Nate Carlton," Sam declared.

There was a rush of noise at the name. "You hail from Texas, the gunman?"

Sam sighed. "Yes, I hail from Texas and I use a gun from time to time."

"You, young fella, where you from?"

"Greenville, up the river."

"Well, no more shooting on this boat, you hear me?"

Two of the crew moved forward to remove the bodies and both Sam and Nate moved to the bar. The cowhand was impressed and offered to buy them both a drink.

"No, friend. I'm obliged to you for backing up my story, so I'll buy you one."

"Well then," the garrulous cowhand offered. "Man'd say you should go careful and watch your back. The man you downed was Chord Wallace, gunman from Cherry Creek and considered mighty salty in some circles. He has some rough friends and news'll spread is all I'm sayin'."

"I appreciate the thought and I'll bear it in mind," Nate responded. And in the back of his mind, he realized that here on this riverboat he had killed his first man, face to face in cold blood, not the heat of battle. It left him with an uneasy feeling in his stomach. Had he been too fast to shoot? No, he had waited until the last second, but the gun had just appeared in his hand as if by magic, with no conscious thought. All the hours of practice had paid off, and he now drew and shot by instinct alone.

Chapter Eight

The next morning Nate felt as empty as ever. The loss of his parents and his childhood home had cut away the moorings of his life, and the shooting had affected him deeply. He stood on the rail and watched the river drift on by, seeking solace in the bubbles of the water that was agitated by the paddlewheels.

He smelled perfume, faint on the air, and turned to see two ladies walking towards him. They were dressed in the height of fashion, yet they were both unfashionably tanned about their faces, a look that spoke of time spent outdoors rather than in some town parlor. By the similarity of their features and the age difference he guessed they were mother and daughter.

The daughter was pretty, with coppery hair shot through by the sun and twinkling blue eyes, and there was a sprinkling of freckles across the bridge of her nose. She was tall and the dress showed off her figure. The mother was darker, but still a handsome woman, who looked like she'd kept herself in trim over the years.

As they approached, Nate raised his hat in polite acknowledgement. "Good morning, ladies," he said.

The daughter smiled, showing even white teeth, and it seemed to Nate that her whole face lit up. She was beautiful when she smiled, he decided, not just pretty.

"Good morning," she replied in cultured tones that sounded northern to his ear, casting her eyes down and nodding to him. But Nate's pleasure was short lived.

"Isobel!" the mother scolded, in a voice that carried. "We do not talk to killers and gunmen. That is one of the men who was involved in the shooting yesterday in the saloon."

The daughter was suitably admonished, and the mother bustled her away before Nate could defend himself or his actions. She half turned to look at him, but her mother tapped her on her upper arm and the girl cast her eyes down once more.

Nate shook his head in disgust, sad at what had occurred. He felt guilty that such a lovely girl had seen him kill a man, and he felt it was unfair that any chance at her company had been so forcefully prevented. The past was slipping away. Not so long ago, he reasoned, he would have been welcomed as a suitor and an eligible bachelor, not seen as just a gun-toting killer. He followed the progress of the two women and saw that the mother left the open air of the deck to enter a private cabin. The girl stood at the rails, looking out over the water, the breeze catching the brim of her dainty hat as she fought to keep it in place.

With the action, her head turned and she caught Nate's

eye, and much to his pleasure she moved in his direction away from the door to her cabin. She blushed as she came nearer, looking to all the world like she was amazed at her own boldness.

"Allow me to apologize for my mother's rudeness. We are from the east, and this violent new world is alien to us. I know from Ned Buntline dime novels that things like this happen all the time and ... well ... I felt that something needed saying..." Here she faltered.

Nate closed the distance until they were a few feet from the cabin door, where they were unlikely to be overheard. The girl—Isobel, her mother had called her—looked over her shoulder, alarmed that her mother might catch her disobeying her command.

Nate removed his hat and offered his most winning smile. "Nathaniel Carlton, ma'am. Think nothing of it and I certainly do appreciate you taking the trouble to talk with me. They call me Nate, and I'm from Greenville, up along the river back there." He motioned over his shoulder and held out his hand. "How do you do?"

"Isobel Hart," she replied. "How do you do?" She held out a gloved hand to him, and he took it. Her light skin couldn't hide her blush, and Nate realized that it made the freckles on her nose stand out more.

Nate realized he was gawping and clutching her hand. He released it and quickly sought to fill the awkward silence. "Are you traveling far?" he said.

"We're visiting relatives of my mother's in Charleston and then heading back up to the northwest, where Papa is hoping to buy a ranch near Langtonville," she replied breathlessly.

"I'll be riding over in that direction myself. Perhaps we shall meet again in more auspicious circumstances." He exaggerated his English accent, hoping to impress Isobel.

Instead, she frowned. "Where are you from?" she asked. "Originally, I mean. That accent has a hint of English, doesn't it? We have friends in Boston who are from the Old Country, and they talk a little like you."

"You have the right of it. My parents are..." He stammered and was momentarily struck dumb. "They were English. We arrived here when I was ten years old so there must be some of it left in my voice. Ma'am, I know that this is terribly forward, but if I was ever in Langtonville would I be able to call upon you?"

"I ... Yes, I should like that. My father's name is Charles Hart. I am sure that you will find us if you ask someone. Hopefully Mother will be more amenable by then, once she has experienced more of the west. She's a mite too concerned for me at the moment, I guess. We're a little out of our depth here. I should go now before she comes looking for me."

Nate barely had time to touch his hat before she was gone, and with her his heart. There was something about her that captivated him, like no other girl he had met. There had been balls at his parents' home before he'd run off to be a soldier, and some of the girls there had been more beautiful than this copper-haired vision, but none of them were quite like her. He had fumbled and laid with the whores who had hung around the camp during the war, as much for comfort as sex, but this was different, and he vowed that he would see her again.

Somehow.

Sam rose late, as he always did when he had the benefit of a comfortable bed rather than a blanket on the trail. He always wanted to make the most of it whenever he had the opportunity. He strolled along the deck looking refreshed and none the worse for his adventures of the previous evening. He wore a black gambler's coat and a neat white shirt with a string tie, much as Abe had the day before.

"Why, Sam, I nearly didn't recognize you all duded up like that," Nate said.

"'Bout time someone raised the standards. We've been on the trail too long, the both of us. I'm lookin' better'n you, anyways. You look a mite peaky. Everything all right?"

"Yes and no. I was thinking about last night and everything. Then it occurred to me. You're heading deeper into South Carolina. It'll be a new country for you, while for me it's still familiar, with all that means. I think I need to break out and head west, Sam, heading into the country that you just left, if that makes sense."

Sam lit a cheroot, striking the match on his heel. He puffed and dragged on the tobacco, squinted his eyes against the smoke and finally said: "I've been expecting it, Nate. Man can't go through what you've been through and not want a change of scene."

They talked it through, and Nate made a decision. "At the next stop I'm getting off and heading west to Texas. I should like to see some of the country over there."

"What will you do?"

Nate shrugged and looked out at the flat countryside through which the boat was making steading progress. "I don't really know what I'll do. Drift along I should think, and maybe get work herding cattle. Seems kind of romantic in a vague sort of way. It's miles from the Mason-Dixon line, so I should find less trouble there, I hope."

Sam arched an eyebrow. "Remember what that cowpoke said last night. Wallace had friends and a brother, as I recall, so watch your back. On that note, thank you for last night. You surely saved my bacon—again!

"And there is something more I can teach you before you go. At least to give you something to practice. The Border Shift now. You're getting there, but you need to learn to shoot with your left hand too. No use shifting gun hands if'n you can't shoot worth a cuss with the weaker hand. You'll find it awkward, but you'll get there with practice."

"Understood. But wait, there was that maneuver you showed me right at the beginning. You know, where you span the gun to face the other way?"

"Ah, the Road Agent's Spin. Okay, watch closely." Sam withdrew his Colt, bringing it out butt forward, pointing the barrel at himself. "Ready?"

Nate nodded and with that the pistol took on a life of its own, spinning around Sam's hand to face Nate, hammer drawn, cocked and ready. It had all happened in a split second.

"Amazing! Show me again, but slower this time."

"Right. You hold the gun like this, butt out, and as you do, curl your trigger finger under the guard and through, in front of the trigger." Sam demonstrated the move slowly enough for Nate to see it. "You let it drop, like so. Now you see it is upside down, like it's halfway through all those pinwheeling spins you've been practicing to get your trigger finger stronger. Then you flip it up like so." He dropped his wrist and the butt seemed to leap obediently into his waiting palm.

"Now you try it with your own gun. You carryin' six loaded chambers now?"

"No. Since you worked on the spur wheel and the mechanism it's so light I don't dare trust myself until I get used to it, so I'm still carrying only five. The pull is so smooth, it's like silk."

"Good. I don't want you shooting your darnfool foot off," Sam mocked him gently. "Or blowin' off some poor lady's hat." He raised an eyebrow and Nate realized that when he'd been talking to Isobel he had taken no notice of anything else—which might be dangerous in the wrong circumstances.

Nate grinned and drew his own gun, butt outwards. He inserted his finger into the trigger guard, at which Sam stopped him and showed him the correct way. "That's it, now let it drop and ... flip."

The first time he failed, but on the third attempt the gun landed a little awkwardly in his palm. "Excellent. At least I know the technique now, and I can work on getting it smooth and fast."

"It will come, especially as you have a natural aptitude for it. But take it easy and only shoot when you need to. That said, there's precious little in the way of law where you're going, save the law of the gun. You mind that, young

Nathaniel, and don't go gettin' caught with your pants down." At which he slapped Nate on the back. "Come on, I'm hungry for breakfast."

A day later they parted company at Heller's Creek boat ramp. It was a sad moment and Nate felt as if another part of him had died. With the horses unloaded, he mounted and reached down to shake Sam's hand.

"Thanks for everything, Sam. I hope to see you along the trail somewhere."

"You take care, boy, and holler if you need me," Sam urged.

Nate looked back one more time and saw Isobel Hart waving from the deck. He waved back and his heart thumped in his chest. Then he pushed the horses into a fast walk and moved away toward a new country and a new life.

Chapter Nine

Nate moved west, skirting Greenville and retracing his steps into the heart of the southwest. At Atlanta, because he disliked carrying so much money around, he opened a bank account where he deposited the gold from his father's safe together with some of the hundred dollar bills. He made an arrangement with them to wire money to any bank of his choosing whenever he needed it. He stored the remaining cash in a new money belt around his waist and folded a hundred dollar bill inside his hatband.

That done, and after a night's rest in Atlanta, he set out on the trail with new supplies, leading Patch, the Appaloosa quarter horse cross, behind the buckskin. Patch was starting to settle down. He allowed a pack saddle without too much complaint or bucking and with gradual and gentle care and affection was starting to accept people again without wanting to kill them. Each night at camp Nate practiced with his gun and trained Patch. He waited until the horse had relaxed and recovered from the day's ride, knowing the old adage that *a fresh horse won't train and a tired horse won't train*, and made him work a little harder each day, lunging him and getting him to respond to his voice and various commands from the ground.

A few days later he made camp in a natural hollow shielded by rocks and trees, with just one entrance into the rough circle. Here he decided that he would try to mount Patch and see if the horse would accept him. Entering the circle, which was about fifty feet in diameter, he tied up both horses, unsaddled them and let them drink from a small stream that dribbled from a fissure in the rocks and puddled in a shallow pool before disappearing into the ground. When they were done, he fitted feedbags to their halters with just a small handful of feed. He didn't want the Appaloosa's belly too full of grain just yet.

Looking around he saw the remnants of a couple of old fires. Clearly this was a likely spot for travelers who knew their way about the country, just off the trail. The stream fed lush grass and it was a peaceful place. With a small fire set near a crop of rock that the windblown sand had eroded to form a crude natural chimney, Nate removed the feedbags from the horses and with a soft voice and calm movements began to curry the Appaloosa.

"Now don't you worry, horse, this is going to be as easy as you make it. I'm not going to hurt you, I just want to settle on your back there," he said, and with these mutterings in the time-honored fashion of every horseman down the ages, Nate settled first the blanket and then the saddle upon the horse's back. Tightening the girth, he let the horse think about it for a while before setting the sweet iron bit in his mouth, warming it first in his hand and adjusting the bridle to the size of his head. That done, he left him lightly tethered to a tree and moved away with a small axe and began to chop down three young trees from outside the circle. These he dragged to the narrow entrance and formed a crude crossbar blocking the exit, using stones as pillars. He now had a barrier just about waist height. Finally, he placed the last bushy trunk in the middle and leant it against the cross.

"That ought to do it," he mused out loud. "Won't stop you if you're determined, but it might dissuade you a little." Then he approached the Appaloosa, whispering gently and untying him. Giving the girth one more hole on the latigo strap, he stepped up into the saddle. He tried to remain calm, but he was still a little tense, expecting an eruption. Nothing happened, Patch stood stock-still, his knees locked. Then, just as Nate leant forward to pat him, he seemed to explode into action. All four feet kicked at once in an enormous buck, lifting them both right off the ground. The landing jarred Nate, who barely held on. Then Patch launched himself onto his front legs, corkscrewing his rear, and Nate flew out of the front door to land jarringly on the crushed grass. He rolled out of the way in case the horse trampled him, lying half raised on one elbow, winded and gasping.

"Damn it, Patch, and we were getting along so well." He chuckled to himself when he'd gotten his breath back. "Well, no one said it was going to be easy, especially after what you went through with Gillett."

Twice more the stallion threw him crashing to the ground and twice more he mounted again. By the fourth attempt he had learned the tricks and twists that Patch put in and sat the bucks and lurches. Finally the bucking stopped, and the horse stood and snorted, shaking his head and walking first one step then another. When he stood still, Nate did not urge him to move but spoke quietly, stroked him and dismounted and offered him a handful of grain from his pocket.

"Well done, boy. Soon you'll be earning your keep and giving poor old Buck a rest," he said.

He stayed for two days in his makeshift corral, and by the third day he judged Patch rideable. In that time, he practiced more with the Border Shift, the Road Agent's Spin and other moves Sam had taught him. His left hand was improving, but he decided that it would never match the right for speed or skill—not that it mattered. Competency was what he was striving for.

He practiced diving, rolling and shooting, firing from his knees and all possible other positions. The pistol had become an extension of himself. It never required active thought, it just came into his hand as if by its own volition. It was a tool to be used, and he wanted to make the best of all the tools that were at his disposal. The process helped Patch to get used to the idea of sudden gunshots at close range.

The following day he saddled Patch, strapped the supplies onto Buck and set off into a beautiful fall morning heading west towards Alabama with the sun at his back through a land of streams, lakes, green pastures, and forests. It was stunning scenery and Nate decided he would come back someday and explore it. He saw all sorts of wildlife, a few small homesteads where he was made welcome and thousands of steers roaming around grazing in small herds.

The days passed, the leaves started to turn to rich golds, reds and ambers and the nights became colder. He rode through the rolling pastures of Mississippi until he came to the great river the state had been named after. Ironically, he arrived back at Greenville but found it different enough from his identically named hometown in South Carolina and crossed the murky, slow river on the ferry, feeling like he was entering a new world when he landed in Arkansas. There, the verdant plains sloped gently up from the mighty river and were so green it looked like something artificial. The soft and welcoming land rose and fell gently. The accents of the farmers and the townsfolk were still Deep South, which he found comforting in a way, and most people were friendly. He came across a few hardcases in some town saloons but avoided their eye, not wanting any trouble. He moved on before anyone could challenge him.

But riding two well bred horses of good stock he was mindful that there were two obvious reasons for waylaying him. Good horseflesh was hard to come by after the war and everyone noticed the quality of the animals he rode, especially the Appaloosa. A squint-eyed man stared at him as he left the ferry planking, and he remembered what Sam had told him about gangs targeting the ferries and lone travelers who offered easy pickings.

As he pulled out of town another rider appeared from his left, also with a baggage mule in tow. They seemed to be taking the same road westwards. After a few miles the newcomer was within hailing distance.

"Hey friend, mind if I join with you? Seems like we're headin' in the same direction."

Nate pulled up and looked around, suspicious at first, but there was no one around that he could see or sense. "Sure, why not?"

He stood sideways on, waiting as the rider approached. "Howdy, I'm Jim Matthews and I'm headin' west." The man smiled.

Nate saw a man in his mid-twenties, raw boned and sporting a mustache that drooped downwards at each side of his lip. A pistol hung at his waist in an old cavalry holster from which he had cut the flap. His boots were a little run down and his denim pants were faded from long use. His smile seemed genuine, and he spoke with a southern drawl.

"Good to meet you, Jim. Name's Nate Carlton. I'm moving west too, don't know how far or where I'll end up. Somewhere in Texas, I guess. I've longed to see the country there."

"Yup, I hear its mighty purty, too. I'm headed for the state border, so if'n that's alright I'll likely accompany you some of the way?"

Nate agreed and they carried on in companiable conversation. As evening fell they found a spot to camp and set to hobbling the horses. Nate kept looking around. Something felt wrong, but he couldn't put his finger on it.

"You alright?" Jim asked.

"What? Um ... yeah. I just can't shake the feeling that we're being followed or watched. I don't know, I'm a mite jumpy, I've been that way since scouting in the war. It never leaves you. Probably just my imagination." Nate shrugged, dismissing the idea.

"I know what you mean. Kinda gets me sometimes, too.

Don't feel nothin' now though, but I'll mind what you say." With that he went off to gather kindling and prepare a fire.

With a small blaze going, the two men set up camp with ease born of long practice. Nate went to his supplies and started to produce the makings of supper, coming back with flour, beans and a side of bacon.

Jim squatted by the fire. Looking up at his arrival, he pushed back his old cavalry cap, scratched his tousled hair and stood as though to help Nate. Holding the hat in his left hand in front of his stomach, Jim masked the actions of the right and clumsily produced a worn Army Colt from the twist draw holster. "Now hold it right there, Nate, and don't do nothin' foolish with that there Colt. There'll be three more guns pointin' your way and they'll be long guns that won't miss. Come on in, boys. I got 'im."

Nate cursed himself for a fool. What had Sam said? *Trust your instinct.* He'd ignored that feeling of unease and now he would now pay the price. He heard rustling from behind and knew that however fast he might be, the deck was stacked against him. With assailants he couldn't even see with rifles at this range he was a sitting duck.

"Better do as he says. We got you dead to rights," came a new voice from cover.

Jim spoke, keeping out of the line of fire. "Now you just put your right hand on your head, that's it, and unbuckle your gun belt with the left and throw it to you right."

Nate complied, making no sudden movements, tossing the new gun belt a few feet away.

Three figures entered the campsite from different directions, two held rifled muskets left over from the war and the third an army Remington .44 that had seen better days.

They were roughly dressed in greasy clothes, and the leader was the pot-bellied man with a squint who Nate had spotted at the ferry. His trousers were held up by suspenders showing from underneath an old leather coat. He held his musket cocked and aimed at him.

"You got 'im then, Jim. Good work. We done found ourselves a pigeon for the pot. Now, bub, what have you got in your trouser pockets and vest?"

In the half-light Nate emptied his pockets of a handkerchief, a clasp knife and a few coins. In his vest they found a wallet with an assortment of bills amounting to just under seventy five dollars.

"Well now, that's a tidy sum, I declare. I reckon with your gun belt and pistol and other gear and them two fine horses we've done ourselves all right, boys." He grinned wickedly at the others.

A weasel-faced man asked: "What're we gonna do with him? Shoot 'im?"

"No. We don't want to look at ourselves on a wanted poster, now, do we? Now you listen here, bub. We're gonna leave you now. We'll take your boots, mind, so you don't get no ideas about followin' us. But don't you get any ideas anyways, 'cause there's no law here ceptin' the law of the gun, and that's the law we make. We see you again we'll shoot you dead. Understand?"

Nate nodded, showing no emotion but seething with anger inside. He knew his life was hanging in the balance. One wrong move and they would kill him out of hand.

"You keep walkin' west, you'll get to Montrose, 'bout ten miles that way." The man nodded to his left. "Mind, it'll take you awhile barefoot." At which they all laughed harshly.

"You really going to take my boots? It's a long way."

"Tough, sonny. Greenhorns like you should stay in the city where they belong. Now we're gonna ride off, we'll leave you the fire for comfort. Remember what I said now, we don't want to see you ever again. Let this be a lesson to you. Now, lever 'em off."

Nate complied and stood there in his socks. With that they packed up the camp and as Jim was walking by he knocked off Nate's new Stetson. "Now I'd admire to have that. My old cap's a tad shabby, but I'll leave it for you as a keepsake. So long, *pardner*."

The others laughed at Nate's discomfort and the group rode off into the night, taking all his gear and the two horses, with Patch pulling and tugging at his rein at the sudden appearance of the strange men. They left Nate there in his stockinged feet, furious and filled with the desire for vengeance. Emotions roared through him like a flood, his fists shaking with anger at his side.

You're all going to die, and I'll laugh as I kill you, he swore to himself, and there was no mercy in him.

As the sound of the hooves disappeared, he found his way back to the main trail cursing with each stone that stabbed into his foot and every thorn that pierced his skin.

Reaching the trail, he looked left and right, then with a pale halfmoon casting enough shadow to pick out the road forward, he headed west. He sighed inwardly. Prudence would dictate waiting until daylight, but that just wasted more time being hungry, cold and thirsty and he wanted to be in the next town by sunup. The road was hard and rutted. His socks initially saved his feet but after a mile or so they wore through. He doubled them over to get another mile or two of protection, but by the time he reached Montrose his feet were cut, bleeding, and bruised.

The town, such as it was, was a one street affair with two saloons, a livery stable, a hardware store, a bank, a few small businesses and some houses. Then he spotted a wooden two-story structure with *Ma's Cafe* printed in shaky capitals on a sign outside at the end of the street, from which came the enticing aroma of coffee and freshly baked bread.

He was light-headed from lack of water and food, hobbling and limping, not sure which foot to favor. Both feet left bloody tracks. Two wooden steps led up to the small veranda in front of the café. Nate missed the second and fell forward, throwing his arms up just in time to break his fall but landing with a thump on the wooden planking. The door opened and a plump woman stood there, hands on her hips.

"Still drunk from the night before, huh? I heard you boys hollerin' 'til all hours. You surely don't deserve no breakfast, not 'til you clean yourself up at least," she berated him.

He looked up, his face tired and grubby with two days growth of beard.

"Ma'am, I do apologize, but it wasn't me hollering. I just walked the best part of ten miles and I'm pretty beat up. I could use a cup of coffee and something to eat," Nate replied from his knees.

"Land sakes, boy, well I'll be. Here, let me help you. Come on in." She sprang forward and with surprising strength lifted him to his feet. He winced in pain as his feet hit the floor again and the woman gasped as she saw the state of them.

"Look at you. What happened to your boots? Let me get you set and I'll bring a bowl and some water. You need to look after your feet 'fore they turn bad with all that dirt." With that she dropped him into the nearest chair and bustled off. She returned minutes later with a bowl of hot water, two towels and some iodine.

"I'm Ma Emma. Leastways that's what everyone calls me, and I'm the closest thing we have to a doctor here, so let me help you out. Now dip them feet of yours slowly into that water. It's hot but it'll do 'em good." She was efficient and clinical, asking no questions and just getting on with nursing his feet, for which Nate was grateful.

The heat was at once soothing and vicious, causing Nate to inhale sharply. It soon became brown with grime and red with blood, and Nate bent forward to rub off all the blood and dirt. When he was done Ma Emma left to fetch a new bowl. When his feet had been washed clean she toweled them off gently and looked up at him. "Now this is going to sting a mite, but it'll save your feet from any poisonin'." She poured a small amount of the iodine ointment over his feet and used a fresh cloth to rub it in. That done she produced some clean bandages from somewhere and wrapped his feet in a professional manner.

"Now you sit tight where you are and I'll get you a cup of coffee and some breakfast." The woman disappeared and returned with breakfast, a full coffee pot and two cups.

"Now tell me everything that happened."

Nate tucked into bacon, eggs and fresh bread and drank numerous cups of coffee. Between mouthfuls he explained what had occurred.

"Sounds like that no-account Zeke Tyler. He damned near runs Greenville, and most folks are afraid of him. Runs with a nasty bunch, and I've long suspected him of being an outlaw. So what are you going to do?"

Nate emptied his mouth, looked up from his coffee cup, stared across at her and said: "Ma'am, I'm going to get myself another outfit, ride over there and kill them all for the horse thieves that they are."

Ma looked at him as his strength returned, seeing the determination and steel under the veneer of manners and breeding that were obvious to anyone who heard him speak. "Yes, I do believe you will. But don't go off half-cocked. Take a day to rest, they'll keep. There is a flophouse down the street but if you want a place to stay with clean sheets, I let out a couple of rooms out the back and you're welcome to take one."

"Ma'am, that's very kind of you, and I can pay. They took everything but they were too stupid to look too hard and they didn't find my money belt." Nate patted his stomach.

"First off you'll need some footwear, and I recommend somethin' soft to ease your feet back in a little. There's an old Cherokee squaw, has a small place out the back of the town. Tribe threw her out for bein' bad medicine. Anyway, she makes all sorts and she'll sell you a pair of moccasins. Darn good they are too."

"I'm obliged to you, ma'am. Now I need to rest, and I'll see that room if I may." Nate realized he was dog tired, and the food had made him sleepy. Also, he wanted to stay out of sight and cause no comment that might get back to Greenville or to Zeke Tyler.

He slept for the rest of the day and when he woke he found a pair of moccasins by his bed. He gently slipped his feet into them.

Coming out for supper, Ma Emma served him. "They fit you all right? They're just readymades, but she's making you a proper pair with wool padding that you can take out later."

Nate thanked her. He wolfed down the food and returned to the room, keeping out of sight. He was surprised to find a couple of books on the shelves by his bed, even more when he saw it was Edgar Allen Poe: *The Murders in the Rue Morgue*. He settled down to read, glad of the peace and quiet, forcing the looming problem that he had to face from his mind and stoking the vengeance that glowed like hot coals in his heart.

Chapter Ten

Two days later he was moving around much more easily. The padded moccasins were beautifully crafted, and he now walked without a limp. He visited the old Cherokee squaw and paid her twice her asking price, so grateful he was for the quality and fast work. She smiled, creasing her seamed face even further as he thanked her in her own tongue. Nate had worked with some Cherokee scouts in the war and knew a few words, which he used to express his gratitude.

He hired a horse and some tack from the livery stable. The horse was a placid but well put together gelding that would get him to Greenville and back with ease. A trip to the hardware store produced a cheap hat and a replacement for the coat that he'd lost to the outlaws. In the gun case he found an old but serviceable Army Colt. This he shoved in his waistband and bought some paper cartridges, ball, powder and percussion caps. He fired a few rounds off in the back target area, and once satisfied he bought the pistol.

Thus equipped, he went back to Ma's, got himself something to eat and set off for Greenville.

He took his time, picking a spot about ten miles outside of the town just off the main trail. He had wanted to tether his horse and sneak around to check the lie of the land. He knew that his feet would still be too painful for an extended walk, and the next day he tethered his horse in a copse a few hundred yards from the town near an old, deserted shack. The door had caved in, and the roof had holes in it, but it would provide basic shelter for him while he figured out what was going on.

Many of the buildings were new, the old town further downriver having been devastated by a raid from the river in which it had been torched by Union soldiers in retaliation for resisting them. The cotton mills outside the town were still very active and bore the names of prominent local families who were thriving on the cotton trade and were now revitalizing the community with new growth and production. Former slaves, now paid for their labor, toiled away, sweating just as hard as they had before the war.

The land was wooded where the cotton plantations had not cleared the growth and was set in a flat basin leading down to the river. New shacks had been thrown up to house workers, and teams of men labored to erect new structures as quickly as possible. The town was slowly but surely rising from the ashes of the Civil War.

Making his way down the main street, Nate saw milling groups of men, the flotsam and jetsam of the western melting pot. They were a rough crowd and would brook no gentle reasoning. It would be guns, fists or knives and no mercy for anyone who crossed them. As Tyler had said, there was no sheriff or marshal's office, and it would be every man for himself. From his hiding place behind the livery barn, he watched the ferry pulling in from across the river, and sure enough he saw the squint eyed features of Zeke Tyler, slouching down by the unloading ramp looking for likely prey among the new arrivals. Nearby stood a man wearing a new black Stetson that was at odds with the rest of his scruffy attire. "That's two of you," Nate muttered, "so where are the other two bastards?"

He saw that neither man was wearing his gun belt. They must have sold it on, unless one of the other two had it.

Considering this, he moved away behind the buildings and walked along the back alley behind the general store, slipping quietly inside. The store smelled of new lumber and paint. A counter ran down one side, and all sorts of goods were on display from food to rolls of material, and next to the hardware section there was a display area. The store-keeper appeared from a back door and smiled at Nate.

"Mornin'," he said. "What can I do for y'all?"

"Good morning. I was wondering if you had any second-hand goods, leather wear, that sort of thing. My old holster was torn off and I'm carrying my gun in my belt."

"Yes, sir, I surely do, right over here."

Nate followed the owner to the array of leather goods, among which hung his new holster and gun belt.

"Where did you get that?" Nate asked, keeping his voice even and his tone free of threat.

"I did a deal with a feller when he brought it in for sale. So I'm sorta selling it for him. Why d'you ask?"

"Because it's my rig, and I was robbed of it three days ago on the trail. If you look inside the belt you'll see the initials of the maker, TT, and then my initials, NSC."

The storekeeper took down the belt and ran his eyes along the inside. There he found the initials as Nate had described. He shrugged: "Don't prove nothin'. You could have sold this and now be making up a yarn to get it back. If you want it back, see the owner."

"Oh, I sure plan to. Who is he?"

"Man by the name of Zeke Tyler, works by the docks. You see him down there, bring him back and we'll sort this out."

Nate did not want Tyler alerted, nor did he want to start trouble with one of the town's citizens. So he complied.

"Sure. But did he leave anything else here? Like a pair of black boots, a saddle, maybe? A Navy Colt?"

The storekeeper, known as Collins, looked embarrassed. He stuttered. "N-n-now just you see here, mister, it ain't my problem. You take it up with him."

"I will, but in the meantime don't go selling that gun belt—or the saddle or boots that you haven't got!" A harshness came into Nate's voice.

He turned on his heel and left the store, crossed the main street and waited hidden in an alleyway opposite. As he had suspected, the storekeeper spoke a few words over his shoulder to someone inside and left the building, heading for the back of the town. Nate followed him, ducking behind the shacks as he went.

Collins did not walk far until he came to a row of roughly hewn new shacks. One had smoke dribbling up from a metal chimney stack. He took a furtive look around and banged on the wooden door, which was opened by the weasel-faced man who had wanted to kill him.

"Collins! What the hell do you want?" a disgruntled man croaked, scratching at his armpit, having clearly just risen. The storekeeper forced his way in, and Nate could imagine the conversation that was going on inside. A minute later the storekeeper left and hurried back to the center of town. Nate let him go then walked obliquely to the door of the shack, avoiding being seen through the dirty window at the front of the building.

He heard voices inside and guessed one of the men would be going to warn Zeke Tyler of his presence in town. Nate bent and picked up a length of firewood that was stacked at the side of the doorway, hefting the timber in his hands ready, standing to the side of the entrance. Just as he had guessed, the door opened and Weasel-face appeared. Nate smashed the end of the log into the middle of his face, breaking his nose in a spray of blood and knocking him cold. He fell back into the cabin with Nate following in quickly, closing the door as much as he could.

The fourth man who had waylaid him was sitting on a bunk bed pulling on his boots. He looked up in fright and amazement, making to grab the pistol on the table by his bed. Nate stood there, letting him do it, giving him the chance. There was murder in his eyes. These men had taken everything, stolen his horses and left him on the trail without even the boots he stood up in. They deserved to hang. The man grasped the gun and as he did so Nate stamped on his arm that was outstretched against the table. The man howled in agony, grabbing the broken limb.

"What the hell, mister, you bust my arm! We ain't got no money," he mewled.

"Yes you have. It's my money and that's my gun you just tried to shoot me with." The man looked up, squinting through the pain.

"You? You from the trail, you came back?"

"Shut up. I need to know where my money is along with the rest of my things. I'm in no mood for lies, I'd just a soon shoot you or have you hanged you for a horse thief. Your choice."

"Zeke and Jim have the rest of your gear. Horses are at the livery barn. That there's your pistol, take it and leave me alone. Take it. I don't want no truck with you. Leave me be."

"You left me for dead on the trail, stole my money, my guns and my horses and now you want mercy? You're murdering scum. You're the one who wanted to shoot me. I reckon you're thinking you should have done, too. Take your dumb friend and get off my trail, and if I see either one of you again I'll shoot you on sight."

Nate picked up his Colt and thrust it into his belt beside the army pistol. Then he walked across to the two muskets leaning up by the wall and smashed them over the bedhead, shattering the stocks. The man looked up from kneeling by his fallen friend to protest but seeing the look in Nate's eyes, he fell silent and bent to attend to the unconscious man.

"Mister," he croaked, "he ain't breathin'. You done killed him when you smashed in his face."

Nate said nothing as he moved out of the cabin. *Two*

down, two to go, he thought. They had robbed him. They'd called the tune and he'd been forced to dance to it. It was a rough country, and if you stole a man's horse you deserved to die.

He returned to the hardware store, where he found Collins serving a farmer with some goods. There were one or two groups of farmers and others milling around and looking at the produce on offer, all occupied with their own business or considering what they were going to buy.

Nate walked quietly to the far side of the store, hidden by racks of goods. He picked his own gun belt off the hook and buckled it around his waist, still unseen by Collins, who had his back to the shop behind the counter. Nate pulled out the Navy Colt and pinwheeled it, checking the balance before dropping it into the waiting holster. He moved quickly out of the store, Collins none the wiser. He stopped, tied down the holster and checked the loads to make sure they were all set with percussion caps. He span the cylinder and dropped the gun back into the holster.

It was now just after midday and work had all but stopped on the building sites and he heard a whistle blow from the cotton mills. The saloons were starting to get busy for the lunchtime trade. Nate looked in on one saloon and pushed open the doors stepping inside to the left, as Sam had done. It was mostly full of former slaves. They looked up as one, eyeing a white man suspiciously in what was their perceived domain.

Nate thought that human nature causes segregation as much as rules and laws, and each creed or color naturally migrates to its own kind. The war had changed very little as far as he could see, and there was just as much division as before. He left and moved to the next saloon, the River Tavern. It was more crowded being close to the docks and sure enough up at the bar he saw Jim Matthews, Nate's Stetson pushed back on his head.

He moved quietly up behind him, keeping out of the line sight of the bar mirror, moving silently on moccasined feet, although the noise from the lunchtime crowd would have drowned out his steps anyway. When he was ten feet behind Matthews, he opened his shirt and pulled out Jim's battered old cavalry cap. He span it through the air to land against Jim's beer glass on the bar, spilling some of the liquid.

"What the hell?" Matthews shouted, and at his cry silence spread through the saloon. Those directly by the side of Matthews moved out of the line of fire, sensing trouble. Matthews span around to the left to face Nate.

"You and those other horse thieving bastards stole my horses, my water and my boots. You took everything I had, including my hat which you're wearing."

Matthews was surprised at first, then he started to look scared. He had pegged Nate for a simple soul who was young and naive and would be long gone if indeed he survived at all. He had not expected him to return to face the threats of Zeke Tyler. This was their town, and no one came up against them here.

"You're mistaken, mister. Don't know what the hell you're talking about."

Others in the barroom were looking on with interest. They all knew that any man in the west who stole a horse was, effectively, sentencing the man he stole it from to a long walk or a slow death. It warranted a summary hanging, and no one had any sympathy for a horse thief.

"You're a liar and I'll prove it. Take off that hat and throw it here."

"No," Jim replied.

"So what's inside the hat band, Jim? You tell me and I'll leave it be, but I'm fast losing patience." Jim licked his lips nervously, saying nothing. "Inside the hat band," Nate continued, "you'll find my initials and a $100 bill."

"Okay," Jim said, making to take the hat off his head with his left hand. "Maybe it is your hat. Let's see." With the movement he covered his right hand, but Nate saw the shoulder rise and the elbow turn outwards as he twisted his hand back to draw the pistol from the cavalry holster. Nate allowed him to initiate the move, and just as the gun cleared the leather he drew in one smooth flash of movement, putting two bullets over Jim Matthews' shirt pocket.

Matthews staggered backwards, dead by the time he hit the bar, and slumped down to the floor. Nate kept the gun in his hand in case anyone else objected to the shooting.

One of the two men near him bent to retrieve the black Stetson. He looked inside and found the folded $100 dollar bill behind the leather band.

"What's your name, mister?"

"Nate Carlton. Inside you'll see the initials NSC."

"Sure enough, that's what's written. I guess it's your hat after all. Seems such a small thing to die for."

At that point the batwing doors to the saloon squeaked open and Nate saw in the mirror that Zeke Tyler had entered. The outlaw hesitated for one second, taking in the scene before him, then started to raise the gun that was already in his hand lying against his thigh. The move was fast, with no need to draw the pistol. As soon as Tyler commenced aiming his gun, Nate dropped and span on his heels, turning to face him, leveling his own Colt at the newcomer. A shot flew past his ear where his body had been half a second before. Nate fanned the pistol, firing off three shots as quickly as he could, a pall of black powder smoke erupting around him.

Tyler's heavy body jerked under the impact, shaking and jiggling like a puppet on a string. He braced his legs, and against all the odds tried to realign his pistol for another shot. With no choice Nate cocked his gun once more and put his final shot through Tyler's forehead, flinging him over backwards to land with a lifeless thump upon the barroom floor. Nate did a Border Shift, pulling the old Army Colt from his waistband ready to cover any new hostilities from the crowd, aware that he had no bullets left in his Navy Colt.

"I'll take my hat if you don't mind." He motioned to the man at the bar, who held it out gingerly. "Just place it on my head if you would."

The man did so. "Much obliged, friend. Now, gentlemen, I'm leaving, peacefully if I can. Anyone tries to stop me will get the same. These were my things and all I wanted was to have them back and see these outlaws punished."

The barman answered. "Ain't no one going to hunt you, mister, but know that Tyler had friends, so you might want to watch your back."

"I appreciate it." Nate nodded. "Now I just aim to get my horses from the livery barn and be on my way."

He moved swiftly backwards from the bar and hurried down to the livery barn where he assumed his own horses would be. The ostler was wary, but agreed to saddle the buckskin for him while Nate reloaded his Navy and went to the hardware store, where Collins looked at him nervously, having heard the ruckus from down the street.

"You set me up, mister. If you do that again I'll come back and ram that Spencer you have there—which belongs to me, by the way—down your throat. Now I'll take my rifle and my boots and be on my way." Once settled, Nate returned to the livery store, mounted Patch and left the town at a trot with the buckskin on a lead rein to pick up the gelding that was still tethered at the shack.

Back at the saloon talk soon welled up as the two bodies were shifted to one side of the room so that custom could carry on again. "What did that young heller say his name was?" one of the dockers asked.

"Carlton, he called himself. Nate Carlton. Don't know the name, but that was some fast and fancy shootin'. I dare say we'll be hearin' his name afore too long—long as he stays alive, that is," answered the man who had passed Nate his hat.

Chapter Eleven

Nate traveled west, making the most of the remaining daylight and aiming to reach Montrose by the evening. He watched his back trail, expecting trouble, but he didn't get that prickly feeling at the back of his neck that he'd developed during the war when something wasn't right. As he rode he thought about the men he'd killed. Four now, since the war, when he had vowed peace—or at least sought it. He realized he was still a little shaky at the after-effects of the gunfight. Four men. Was he turning into a cold-blooded killer? There were plenty of those where he was headed, he knew that much, but he still felt remorse. They had stolen his horses, and this was part of life in the west, but his actions had been retribution, not revenge. He hadn't asked to be robbed. Out here he was beginning to realize it was the survival of the fittest, which justified his actions in his own mind.

As the sun dropped toward evening he rode down the main street of Montrose heading for the livery barn.

Arranging for the horses to be cared for, he returned the gentle gelding to its owner and made his way to Ma's café.

He opened the door to a tinkle of the bell and stood looking inside, carrying his Spencer in one hand. He still wore his moccasins as they were so comfortable. There were just two men in the café when he entered, cowhands by their dress, eating at one of the tables. The one facing him nodded a friendly greeting.

"Howdy, mister. Ma's in the back, I guess she'll be out soon." He spoke in a gentle Texas drawl that Nate had heard so often in the war.

"Thank you, I'm much obliged."

Ma Emma appeared carrying a coffee pot in her hand. "Well, now, lookee here. The prodigal returns." She smiled, tilting her head questioningly to one side. "Did you get it sorted, son?"

"I did, thank you," Nate answered gently.

"Well, I'm right pleased to hear it. Need a room for the night?"

"Yes please, ma'am."

"Well set yourself down and I'll get you some food. These two gents are from Texas, but I ain't gonna hold it against 'em." At her words the two cowboys whooped at her, showing how proud they were of the Lone Star State.

"Sit with us, friend, if you've a mind to. I'm Billy Jo, this here's Frank."

"Nate Carlton, how do you do?"

They shook hands and Nate sat down.

"Traveled far?"

"I'm originally from Greenville in South Carolina, then

had to travel back to the local Greenville, and now I'm on my way west. What about you boys?"

"We just been doin' a chore for our boss and we're headed back home to Texas. We're about to go on a big round-up come the spring, pushing a big herd north for brandin' and such. If'n you're lookin' for work later, there'll be plenty over San Antone way. Randall's figurin' on pushin' a herd north to feed all them damned Yankees at some point too. Me, I'd as soon let 'em all starve," he joked.

"You'll get no argument from me there. Where did you serve?" Nate asked. The conversation progressed to talk of the war, with a close bond of fellowship that can only be forged through fighting against a common foe. At length Nate changed the subject, wanting to move on and try to forget it all if he could.

"Tell me, who is this boss of yours?" Nate asked.

"Feller by the name of Randall. David Randall, owns a spread of ten thousand acres or so, the DR Connected. Built it up from nothing, fighting Comanches and everything else along the way. He's a good man and a fair one. Tough, mind, takes no prisoners. Anyways, there's a lot of free cattle all unbranded roaming around and he's rounding 'em all up to sell. Be a big herd by the time he's finished." Billy Jo spoke with pride in his voice as any cowhand did who rode for the brand. "There are some smaller spreads around, and he figures to form some kind of collective and try to take a large herd of as many head as possible north.

"The smaller local spreads benefit and he gets more men in the saddle. Kinda makes it safer all round. Anyways, he pays on the hoof and passes it on to the others once they're sold and he's back in Texas. It'll be tough, mind, what with injuns and herd cutters."

"That sounds interesting. I might just ride along that way and join you. I had no particular plans, and a friend of mine said it was lovely wild country over in Texas, so I ought to take a look."

"Why it's the prettiest country you ever did see. We got all kinds of scenery and some of the longest blue-green grass ever," Frank enthused.

Nate had never known a Texan yet who wasn't proud to let everyone know how wonderful the Lone Star State was. He could not resist a tease. "Now I thought that the blue-green grass came from Kentucky?"

There were immediate howls of derision and denial from the two cowboys.

In the friendly way of most Texans he had met, Nate was immediately included in the company and persuaded to join them when they left in the morning.

"That's mighty kind of you," he said. "I'd be delighted to tag along and keep company with you. I'm not sure I'll go all the way there yet. I might stop off at some of the towns and see the sights."

Nate felt easier in their company. These were not the kind of men to waylay him like the Greenville crowd. There was safety in numbers, and maybe he could relax a while on the trail. They were heading for the saloon, but Nate turned in early, wanting a rest and an early night. They arranged to meet for breakfast and head west together.

The following morning Nate was up with the sun, and on rising he checked his feet. They were healing well and were nowhere near as tender as they had been. With this in mind he eased on his boots and found he could stand without too much discomfort. Frank and Billy Jo arrived shortly thereafter, a little bleary-eyed but ready for breakfast and the trail.

"You boys look like you had a fine time of it last night," Nate commented raising his cup in salute and sipping his tea.

"Ain't nothin' that a pot of coffee and some bacon, eggs, and pancakes won't cure," Billy Jo responded, reaching for the pot to pour a drink. He spluttered as he saw the light colored liquid emerge.

"What in the hell is this?" he demanded.

"It's tea, and it won't help you." Nate grinned. "I drink it whenever I get the chance and I still prefer it to coffee."

"Tea? What the blazes is wrong with you, man? I declare only women drink tea," he chided.

"I'm English, so I've been granted a special dispensation," Nate responded, patting his pockets as though looking for a letter of permission.

"Damn it, I knew there was something off about your accent. We'll be travelin' with a dad-blasted foreigner." Billy Jo smiled, winking at Frank.

"Well at least we won that war. Hope you're around next fourth July, you can help us celebrate!" Frank laughed.

"Oh no," Nate answered, entering into the spirit of the conversation. "We gave it to you, decided it wasn't worth the effort of keeping it. Just a few lumps of rocks and mountains a long way away and a handful of troublesome colonials."

The laughter that followed raised Ma from her kitchen. "What's all this noise so early in the morning?" she complained, arriving with fresh pot of coffee. She'd heard about the escapades of the two cowboys in the saloon the previous evening on the town grapevine and she was surprised they were up and about so early.

"Randall wants us back as soon as we can get there, and he ain't the most easygoing of men. So we figured to make an early start and skedaddle back to work."

With breakfast finished, Nate paid Ma Emma for the room.

"Come back and see me when you're passin' through, Nate. Don't be a stranger—and don't let these yahoos lead you astray." She shook a finger at the two Texans.

"Yes, ma'am, I'll take care, and thank you for everything." With that he raised his Stetson, mounted, and the three men hit the trail.

They continued west, skirting to the north of Louisiana border country, the rolling plains of lush grass stretching out just as far as the eye could see. Swamps and rivers cut through the landscape, and from time to time they crossed them where the bridges were still in place or forded them where they needed to. After a hard day's ride they camped by a small river that bubbled and gurgled south through the landscape. It was shady and cool after a day in the sun, and there was plenty of dry wood for a good fire.

With a camp made and a stew cooking the three sat around drinking cups of coffee. "It certainly is a pretty country. So green and lush," Nate commented.

"Yep, that it is and no mistake. Course, the closer we get to Texas the better it'll get," he joked.

"You Texas boys, I don't know. You'll tell the biggest

windies going. Now, much as I'd like to hear about how wonderful Texas is, I have some practicing to do. Here's a thought—the man who told me and indeed taught me how to use a gun came from Texas, so it must be the right thing to do," he offered with a grin, standing and fastening the cord around his leg to secure his holster.

"I've been wondering about your rig," Frank said. "It looks mighty fine. Did this here Texan have anything to do with it?"

"He did. His name was Sam Kennedy. He helped me a lot and I was sorry to say goodbye, but he went on down the river to New Orleans. He—"

"Sam Kennedy the Texas gunman and ranger? He taught you how to shoot? Were you pards with him? I heard there was a ruckus south of here on a riverboat."

"I remember it," Billy Jo cut in. "Friend of mine, another cowpuncher, was in the bar and saw the whole thing, said there was two men, Kennedy and another. Fastest thing he ever saw, got the drop on Chord Wallace. Yes, that was it." Billy Jo snapped his fingers. "Lon said the man's name was Nate Carlton."

Both men looked expectantly at Nate, who shrugged. "Alright, I was there, but I'd rather not talk about it and would appreciate it if you didn't spread it around. I don't want a reputation as a gunman, I was just helping out a friend."

"Sure, Nate, sure. Gee, you must be fast to have beaten Wallace."

Nate sighed, uncertain now, yet he knew that he needed to practice every day like Sam had told him until it really became so ingrained that he need never think. He had to keep up his speed, if not get faster still. Sighing, he went to a clearing beyond the trees where he began to practice his draw. Again and again, in one fluid motion. Then the Border Shift, as he had done in the saloon. It all came so naturally now. There was no thought, just movement as soon as his brain said *Go!*

"Man, you're fast. I'd never have believed it. No offence but you just look normal not some hard eyed gunman, with a swagger."

The night of the house fire when he knew he'd lost his parents came back to him and he was deep in thought. He had tried to forget, putting it out of his mind. But the thoughts returned, causing bitterness in his soul. Had Gillett died in the fire in a drunken stupor? Should he have gone back and killed him for sure? No, that would make him as bad as any other killer. Then he was aware that Frank was speaking: "I was going to challenge you to a contest, shooting cones or targets, but you'd win hands down."

Billy Jo interrupted. "Say, I've got an idea. I saw one of the boys back home do this."

On a log twenty feet away, he set two large fir cones, six feet apart. Both Frank and Nate were puzzled.

"How the hell does that help, Billy Jo?" Frank said.

"Wait for it. Okay, Nate, you face away from the target so you have to spin, draw and fire, while Frank's facing it." Billy Jo grinned at his deviousness.

"Really?" Nate queried, thinking back to the saloon with Tyler. But he'd seen his man in the mirror and he was much larger target. "Oh hell, why not, just for fun. I'm game if you are, Frank."

"Sure, why not?"

"Okay, then," Billy Jo said. "I'll call it. Nate, you turn around, and when you're both ready let me know and I'll fire my pistol in the air. Neither of you will see me, so it'll be fair."

The two men stood five feet apart, and Nate turned to face away from the target, feeling the adrenaline surge through him. He forced himself to calm down, hearing Sam's words in his head. *Breathe deeply, let your breath out slow and calm yourself down. Get yourself all wound up and you'll make a mess of it. You'll be too fast for your own good.* On the second breath he muttered quietly, "ready". A few seconds later Billy Jo fired his Colt in the air. Nate started to spin, dropping as he had in the saloon and somehow the turning action helped him to focus and draw. It also meant that in a real situation, he presented a smaller target to his adversary.

The crash of two shots sounded almost simultaneously, Nate shading Frank by a millisecond. But Nate's bullet missed the target, hitting the bark next to the cone while Frank shattered his pinecone to oblivion.

"Damn you're fast, Nate. You shaded me even when you had to turn, focus, and fire," Frank exclaimed.

"Yeah, but I missed the cone," Nate replied, trying to hide his disappointment.

"I wouldn't want to be anywhere near that cone if'n you shoot like that," Billy Jo added, shaking his head. "If that cone was a man you'd have plugged him someplace."

"Well, it was fun and gives me something to aim for. Spin and try to hit the target," Nate offered modestly. "But mind you keep it to yourselves boys, for my sake. I don't want a reputation as a gunny for some young trigger-happy reputation hunter coming after me."

"Sure, Nate, I understand," Frank agreed as he looked over at his new trail partner. Something he knew was driving that young man. No one practiced like that and became that good without a reason. Somewhere, at some time, something had gone wrong for him. But he figured it was none of his business, so he let the matter drop.

Then Nate had an idea. "Can we try that again?" he asked. "This time I want to put my gun in my belt and try a cross draw."

The two other men grinned at each other. "Sure. Let's give it a whirl," Frank said. Nate reloaded his Navy, inserting a spare, fully loaded cylinder into the gun, that he rotated to balance wear and tear, spinning it out of habit.

Billy Jo set up two new cones, and this time Nate pushed the gun loosely into his belt, with the butt facing towards his right hand. "Ready!" he called.

The pistol shot sounded. Nate span and Frank drew, and this time Nate hit the cone. "Woo hoo! Nate, you did it," Frank said. "Man, that was pretty fancy. Interesting how it works better on the cross draw. You'll have to git yourself another gun and holster." Frank slapped him on the shoulder.

The words gave a grinning Nate food for thought. Maybe having a set up like Sam's would be a good idea after all.

Chapter Twelve

As the journey continued the three became firm friends, and soon the daily gun practice was no longer considered a novelty. Nate found himself in a strange position of showing the other two some of the moves that Sam had taught him. But more importantly, when Frank and Billy Jo found out that he could read and write, they expressed an interest and asked if he'd mind teaching them. He agreed readily, pulled out a battered copy of *Bleak House* and began showing them the letters, drawing them in the dirt. In return he asked them a favor.

"Now I know that you are probably going to think I'm stupid, but maybe you can help me out with something."

Frank and Billy Jo looked at each other in puzzlement, wondering what on earth Nate was going to ask them. "Fellas, I can ride and everything, but no one ever showed me how to rope a cow. If I'm going to get a job working on a ranch, I guess I'll need to know how to do it."

The two Texans looked at each other aghast. They had

never considered the idea that Nate couldn't rope. They'd both been doing it since they could walk.

"Land sakes, Nate, I never thought about it," Frank said. "Sure we can, no problem at all. We'll teach you to rope and you'll teach us to read and write. Seems like a mighty fine arrangement to me."

Upon such terms good friendships were made and bonded. They carried on westwards, and as the two cowboys' learning increased, so did Nate's ability with a lariat. He started to perfect a hooley-ann throw for dropping cattle by picking up their knees.

"You'll need it come branding time," Billy Jo remarked, "because you sure as hell don't want to be wrasslin' a cow to the ground every five minutes. Just drop 'em, hog tie 'em and off they go."

They crossed the Texas state line and left Mount Pleasant behind them, making for Dallas. The huge prairie stretched out before them, the flatland broken by rocks and small mountains, rivers and knee high grass that supported cattle herds or buffalo. It was an amazing sight to see the big, shaggy-headed beasts rolling along, unworried and unstoppable. A dust cloud followed them along with the raw stench of dung and the intense aroma of wild animals. It was a primeval scene laid out before them, like nothing Nate could ever have imagined.

"That sight will stay in my mind forever. I feel privileged to have seen it," Nate declared, wanting to get closer to the vast herd, yet not wanting to scare them.

"You won't scare 'em much, not unless you holler and start shooting off your pistol. They don't pay anyone much mind. The odd coyote might try and pick off a straggler or a young 'un but apart from that there's safety in numbers. That big old bull there..." Frank pointed to the largest animal Nate had ever seen. "He'll give you no change from a dollar happen you want to tackle him."

"Good eating, too," Billy Jo added. "We could drop one for some grub happen we was hungry. Need to get it right, though, just behind the shoulder."

Nate pulled his Spencer, dismounted and took careful aim at an older male that was lame and lagging behind. He took a deep breath, exhaled and squeezed the trigger. The animal never knew what hit him. He just crumpled as his last breath left him. The rest of the herd moved on, ignoring their fallen comrade, oblivious to the threat to their way of life as one of their number fell by the wayside.

The three men rode up to the dead buffalo. He was fully grown but there was something wrong with his hind leg. An old fracture perhaps, one that hadn't mended straight. He would have fallen to a predator anyway. Nate thought it sad to see the once proud bull downed in ignominious death. They dismounted and set to skinning the animal, taking two choice cuts of meat for their own needs. Frank made neat work of separating the hide from the carcass with his skinning knife and rolled it roughly into a bundle.

"We'll stake it out next time we stop and dry it off. It'll cure nicely for a coat. Keep you warm in the winter."

"For me?"

"Sure. You're the one who shot it. I'll show you how to cure it," Frank said.

For two more days they traveled slowly, living off buffalo

steaks, taking their time and stopping for longer than necessary to let the hide cure a little. When they reached Dallas, they were ready for a hot bath and a change of diet. Nate had been riding Patch and the buckskin alternately, and he found to his delight that the young Appaloosa was turning into a fine horse and was taking to cutting practice like a natural. They approached the large town with some anticipation. It'd been a while since they'd last been anywhere that felt like civilization. Dallas was bustling and lacked the rundown feel of so many southern towns.

"They had a huge fire here just before the war in '60, nigh on everything has been rebuilt since then," Billy Jo pointed out. "Looks pretty good, don't it? Lots going on."

"Best be careful, though, they got black townships springing up and there ain't no white man safe after dark. Stick to the main parts of the town," Frank added.

"Extraordinary place, so vibrant," Nate offered, seeing the smart two- and three-story buildings, stores, saloons, and restaurants.

The town seemed to be divided up into different sections containing shops, stalls, liveries, saloons, and hotels, while the commercial district boasted banks, lawyers and offices. There was even a sheriff's building, which comforted Nate a little after his adventures in Greenville. The law was here, he thought. The streets were crowded and all shades of life were present. After the quiet of the prairie, it was noisy and lively to the three young men. "What drives all this?" he asked his companions.

"Well, it's one of Texas's main towns," Frank replied. "There's buffalo hunters bringing in hides. Cotton comes down here, too. They started sending it here when the war got closer. Factories and suchlike. Pretty much everything you could ask for and plenty more you didn't even know 'bout. Me, I like it for a day or so, then I have to get out. Too damn noisy and dirty. But they sure do have purty girls in the saloons."

They stabled their horses in one of the livery barns and made for one of the hotels recommended by the liveryman. Registering at the desk, they dumped their gear and headed for the bathhouse at the back. Frank disappeared for a while, saying he had a chore to do.

"Well now, this beats the cold river water for a bath and no mistake. Now I need to get myself some clean clothes to match," Nate commented.

"Plenty of stores for that. We'll get to it once we're all spruced up."

Ten minutes later Frank returned looking a little sheepish but undressed and jumped into the waiting tub. Nate thought nothing more of it.

They got dressed and headed for a general store. Nate bought a couple of shirts, a town suit and some shoes. His new gun belt felt conspicuous in his town clothes, but this was Texas, and the other two told him every man goes dressed and ready down here.

"Hell, it ain't just the men. Damn nearly every man, woman and child carries. It's the Second Amendment and I say amen to it," Frank opined.

Nate liked his new friends, and for all their garrulousness and pride in Texas they were good company and had taught him a lot. Looking around the store he saw various holsters and weapons for sale before something else took his eye. He had heard of them from Sam, but he hadn't seen any before. The display holster was made of soft leather with shoulder straps in a figure of eight configuration, and in it was a new Colt Police Model with a short 3.5-inch barrel. This could be just what he'd been looking for. It would feel the same as his Navy, with an identical grip and caliber, but it would be easy to conceal and therefore less conspicuous. He took down the holster and tried it on. Frank and Billy Jo came over after looking at other goods.

"What are you doing with that itty bitty gun, Nate? Damned if my own sister wouldn't scorn that, 'cept when she was going target shootin' on a Sunday after church," Billy Jo said.

Nate defended his choice. "I like it. It's not heavy and doesn't show under my suit. I can be a city dude now and give you even more reason to laugh at me," he responded good naturedly. "And I might even impress your sister," he added to Billy Jo. Putting on his jacket he looked in the mirror and saw that it hardly showed underneath the coat. "I think it'll take the same ammunition as my Navy, and it might do well as a belt gun for a cross draw."

"Well, just you make sure you don't use it with me around, I'd have to disown you as an Easterner," Frank chided.

Their purchases completed, they headed for the Texas Lady saloon.

The saloon was a three story building and reputed to be the best bar in town, with a restaurant, gambling, and live entertainment. The three men entered to bright lights and a crowded bar that seemed home to all the flotsam and jetsam cross section of the west. There were townsmen, buffalo hunters, cowboys, and gamblers of every shape and size, and all eyes were glued to the stage. A well-tuned piano and guitar played a melody for a singer whose performance was attracting the attention of everyone in the room. She was young, and very pretty. Her blonde hair was piled up on her head, adding inches to her medium height and accentuating her lithe figure. She used her hands and body expressively, adding to the allure of the song, and all eyes were on her as she used the red dress and long black evening gloves to great effect. Everyone in the bar was entranced by her performance, not just because she could sing well, but because women were few and far between and good looking young women who could sing and move like this one were something of a rarity.

The three men stood just inside the door, not daring to move, their eyes fixed on her as she performed, pulling at the heartstrings of every male watching. The singer finished her performance to rapturous applause and curtsied in different directions. In the swell of the applause, she caught Nate's eye and smiled at him for a heartbeat before moving on. It that moment Nate was smitten. He stood stock-still, unable to move.

Billy Jo broke the spell. "Oh my, she sure is pretty," he declared between whoops of approval from the rest of the crowd.

The spell broken, the three moved to the bar, keeping the singer in sight all the way as she accepted the plaudits of the crowd. They ordered a pitcher of cold beer and Nate looked off to the side area, where the restaurant was sectioned off by pillars with drapes and hangings and latticework barriers that still gave a view of the main saloon but offered a more genteel atmosphere in which to eat. He was reminded of a dining room in a gentlemen's club, with padded seats and tablecloths.

"Boys, I'm starving, and I'm fed up with our cooking, I'm off for something better than buffalo steaks and beans."

"We'll catch you later," Frank replied, still staring at the singer. "Me, I'm enjoying the view right here."

Nate moved across, taking his beer with him, careful to avoid spilling it as he went. He looked up at the stage, seeing that the woman in the red dress was about to start another song, and bumped into a man who was applauding the performance.

"Sorry about that," he apologized, offering the man a smile.

"Why don't you watch where you're going, mister? You damn near soaked me!" The man snarled. He was a buffalo hunter, and by the smell of him he was fresh off the trail and hitting the whisky hard. His buckskins were stained and worn, his lank hair long and greasy from lack of attention and he smelled of sweat, blood and death. He blocked Nate's path.

"Mister, I'm sorry and I've apologized. Now, all I want is a peaceful meal and a quiet drink. I want no trouble, so just leave me be, all right?" Nate said calmly.

"No, you owe me a drink and I'll take that beer." The man leered, standing closer, now just a foot away and reaching for Nate's glass. He was looking for trouble and was being egged on by three other similarly clad men at his table, who grinned knowingly.

Nate had seen it around the army camps. Men who worked hard all week, facing death often, came to town tired with a need to let off steam, get drunk and fight. It was the way of the world out here. It was a tough land and it bred tough men. The hunter was big built and raw boned, the hard, tanned planes of his face showing no grace or forgiveness. He had a knife at his belt and a pistol showed in his waistband. Nate knew it was a fight he wanted. He was looking to smash and destroy and let off steam. The crowd around started to quieten in expectation of conflict in the way of men everywhere. But there was anger building in Nate, a lack of tolerance for bullies twisted by recent experiences had left him short of patience.

The foul breath of the man before him billowed out as he spoke. "I don't care what you want, sonny, you shouldn't be drinkin' with men, so I'll take your beer and you can go order yourself a soda pop." The table of his cronies roared with laughter, aware that the young and smartly dressed townsman before them was going to get pummeled come what may.

The two bouncers at either end of the bar looked on expectantly, ready to intervene and force the men outside if anything serious occurred. Their boss did not want a fight busting up his smart saloon, but a small fight always drew attention and added entertainment for the customers.

"Oh, you mean this beer?" Nate asked innocently, speaking calmly and holding his glass up.

"That's the one, sonny." The buffalo hunter grinned

back at his companions and winked, enjoying humiliating the young man before him, who seemed clueless and harmless.

"Well, I guess it's all yours, then." As he turned back to face him, Nate threw the beer into his face and brought the rim of the heavy jug crashing into the bridge of his nose, which broke.

The hunter cried out in pain, bringing both hands to his stinging eyes and broken nose, as he did so Nate kicked him hard between the legs and he dropped to floor in a heap, clasping his crotch, bent double and mewling in pain.

Turning, Nate pulled the gun from his shoulder holster and covered the four remaining skinners. It was not a particularly fast move, he was unpracticed in the draw, having just purchased the weapon and the shoulder holster. However, the unexpected action was in sharp contrast to his timid demeanor and shocked the men before they could think of pulling their own weapons. There was silence in the bar from all who saw the drawn gun.

"Now," Nate began in harsh tones. "I'd be obliged if you gents would just sit there and let me mind my own business. I intend to go get a meal and have myself a peaceful evening. If I see your faces near me, I won't chat with you, I'll just shoot you. Do we understand each other?"

They all nodded in shock.

"Good, Now take this worthless piece of buffalo dung outside." He pulled up the skinner's head by his greasy hair, pointing the gun in his face. "You come for me, or lay for me back-shooting, mister, I'll kill you. You got that?"

The skinner nodded his head, blood pouring from his nose.

At the bar Frank and Billy Jo were looking at the crowd, their pistols drawn to make sure no other buffalo hunters tried to help the four men. They had only seen the friendly, easy-going side of their new companion and were nearly as surprised as the skinners at the transformation before them.

Nate's face was a mask of granite, the features cast in hard and inflexible lines. He gave a final look at the remaining skinners and continued to the dining area, his gun free, the hammer cocked ready. Once through the archway he relaxed slightly, releasing the hammer slowly and holstering the weapon. He felt the tension ebb from him as he realized he had not yet become a heartless killer, despite the bitterness inside him. He knew that some would have shot the hunter without compunction at the provocation. He found a table and sat down, aware of eyes on him from all around the room.

The waiter arrived, well trained and showing no undue interest, and asked if Nate would like a drink.

"Do you have any wine?"

"We do, sir, I shall bring you the list." He moved smoothly off to fetch it. When he returned to Nate's surprise he found an extensive menu with many French dishes that he had knowledge of from home. He chose lamb shank braised in red wine with sautéed potatoes and greens, together with a bottle of pinot noir. The waiter seemed pleased with his choice and bustled off.

In silence as the dinner chatter grew around him he felt the adrenaline slowly leave his body. He realized he was going to have to be careful or he was liable to kill someone in every town he visited. He knew he stood out from the crowd. His mannerisms were refined, his class showed and done up in his town best he looked nothing like he really was. He'd be a target wherever he went if he didn't make the effort to blend in more.

His thoughts were disturbed by his sense of smell, as with bustle of silk he caught the scent of a rich perfume nearby and saw that the singer was moving near to his table making for a secluded part of the dining room. She looked in his direction and smiled.

"Good evening, ma'am," Nate said, standing up to greet her. "You have a fine voice and that was a lovely song."

"Why thank you, kind sir." She gave him a look from beneath lowered lashes. The voice when she spoke was not that of a southern belle, but the accent was northern, maybe New York or Chicago, he was too inexperienced to tell. What he did notice was that she was even prettier close to and avoided the heavy caking of make-up so often adopted by saloon girls.

"If it's not too forward of me, would you care to join me for dinner?" he offered, blushing slightly.

"That is kind, but I already have a dinner date who'll be along shortly," she replied, declining his offer but softening her refusal with a smile.

"Of course, my apologies," Nate replied. The singer hesitated, impressed by his grace and manners.

"But maybe I can sit with you for a few minutes until my date arrives." She diverted her course and Nate pulled out a chair for her and watched as she settled herself with a swish of silk before sitting back down. She thanked him for his courtesy. "That was quite a show that you put on out there," she continued. "And I thought you showed great restraint. Those skin hunters always come looking for trouble and get liquored up ready to take someone apart. It seems to be their Friday night ritual, and I am glad that you didn't get hurt."

"No, ma'am—"

"Caz, Caz Prideaux .She offered him a gloved hand, which he took.

"Nathaniel Carlton. Nate. Like I said, I am sure it was just a misunderstanding, a little too much whisky, perhaps, and a tad over-enthusiastic."

She offered a sweet, mellifluous laugh. "Well now, I have heard that big ox been called some things before, but over-enthusiastic hasn't been one of them." Her laughter broke the ice of formality and they fell into a convivial conversation.

"You're not from Texas. Much further north, am I right?" he ventured.

"You guessed it. I'm one of those terrible Yankees, but don't tell anybody or they might think I'm a spy." Her humor was infectious, and Nate felt himself relaxing. "Chicago originally, via New York and now here I am." Caz spread her hands elegantly.

"That sounds quite a story. I'd love to hear more," he probed.

"Well, my father was an opera singer. He toured all over the world and when my mother died I went with him. We visited Europe, where he sang in many of the capitals."

"London?"

"Sure. We visited there two or three times. Why do you ask?"

"Well by the smallest coincidence that is where my family is from. I was born and grew up there."

"I knew that there was something off about your accent. So you're one of those terrible colonists who lost the war back in '83?" She laughed again.

"No, no," he protested, slipping back into an English accent. "We decided that it wasn't worth all the effort and gave it to you as a present." Their laughter was interrupted as a handsome and well-tailored figure approached their table.

"My dear, I do hope that you're not keeping this young man from his dinner?"

"No, not at all. We were just comparing notes on London. Brad, this is Nate Carlton. Nate, Brad Dexter, owner of the Texas Lady."

"How do you do?" Nate replied, standing once more and offering his hand to the handsome man before him. He saw that he was of medium height but thick set with broad shoulders and a strong face. His hair was slicked back, and a dark mustache graced his upper lip. His clothes were expensive and set off well by a fancy silk vest sporting a gold watch chain. The man looked powerful and ruthlessly confident. Nate took an instant dislike to him but smiled genially.

"Your story will have to wait, I'm afraid." Dexter bestowed Nate a smile that was all teeth and no humor. "Our supper awaits, and the lady has to be back onstage in an hour." He put a proprietorial hand on Caz's shoulder, at which she rose, a slight frown flitting across her face.

"Do excuse me," she said. "It was lovely talking to you. We must do so again and talk more of Europe."

"A pleasure to meet you both." Nate inflected his words carefully, offering them a smile. As he sat back down his two friends arrived carrying a glass of beer each.

"Man, you sure don't waste any time for someone who's new in town. You get into fight with old Jake and then start sparkin' the prettiest girl in the room—an' all before supper. We'll have to watch him, Frank, he may not be able to rope worth a damn but he sure can wrassle up some action when he's of a mind," Billy Jo joked.

Nate couldn't resist his friend's humor and laughed at the break in the atmosphere. "Well, you two old cowpokes, there is a fine menu here if you have a mind to try something other than beef and beans."

Nate's wine arrived.

"What in the hell is that?" Frank demanded, picking up the bottle and examining its dark contents.

"Good French wine, my friends." Nate raised his glass with a grin as Frank and Billy Jo looked at the waiter with suspicion and ordered steak and potatoes with greens.

The rest of the evening passed without incident, and after supper the three of them moved back to the bar to hear Caz sing again in her final call.

Chapter Thirteen

The following morning, feeling a little the worse for wear from the previous night, they walked through the town looking for breakfast and found a café open with the smell of frying bacon wafting through the air. With the grease and eggs mopping up the alcohol, the two Texans made to leave, saying that they had to get back to the ranch. But before they did so, they took Nate to a leather worker who plied his trade in the working quarter. Billy Jo explained as they entered the shop.

"Frank and me, well we've been thinking, and we've decided that if you're going to be an adopted son of the Lone Star State, you can't go round in them shiny cavalry boots. So we're gonna get you a pair of proper cowboy boots. If you're plannin' to stay on for a few days, they'll be ready for you before you move on."

"Boys, I am really touched, that is so kind of you," Nate responded, humbled by their generosity.

"Think nothin' of it, we all's grateful for you for

teaching us how to read and write, but not a word to the boys if'n you ever get to the spread. It would be a mite embarrassin', if you catch my drift," Frank said.

"I do indeed, and if you could keep quiet about my gun skills I'd appreciate it. I'm not looking for any trouble. All I want is to be left alone so I can seek a new life."

"Amen to that. Although I'm bound to say trouble seems to follow you around just a mite too close for comfort. You be careful of those buffalo hunters now, they won't forget what you did and they won't give you an even break. Those Sharps they use carry a long way and I'd advise you to leave town quietly if you don't want a hole in your back."

They shook hands and made to get their horses from the livery barn.

"You take care now, Nate, and we'll see y'all along the trail in San Antone," Frank said.

"I'll be there for the winter and spring round up. I might even have learned how to rope by then," Nate replied.

"Doubt it, but you never know," Frank scoffed. With that they tipped their hats and nudged their horses away down the main street, heading southwest for San Antonio.

Nate was sad to see them go. They were good company, and in many ways he had learned as much from them as he had given by teaching them to read and write. He shook his head at their generosity and walked back to explore Dallas some more.

He was enjoying his time in the large town that was clearly expanding at a rate with new commerce erupting all around him. He walked aimlessly through the streets, looking at the shops. By lunchtime he was hungry again with the kind of hunger that comes from too much whisky, and he sought out the Texas Lady saloon again to sample something else from their excellent menu.

He arrived this time from the side door that led directly to the restaurant, for customers who wanted to avoid the rougher saloon. It was busy with midday trade and the dining room buzzed to the hushed sounds of voices and the tinkle of glasses and cutlery. There was just one table available, and he ended up being seated close to another that was occupied by a single man who was studying a newspaper. He looked up over halfmoon spectacles as Nate sat down and a young couple descended on the table he had just secured.

Seeing the congestion, the occupier of the neighboring table spoke to him in well-modulated tones. "If you don't mind sharing my table you'd be welcome. I always enjoy company and I'd be happy to buy you a drink for the pleasure of yours."

Nate was not quite sure why he accepted the man's invitation. Maybe it was because of the recent loss of his talkative friends or maybe because he was interested in people and wished to pass the time in convivial conversation, which from his opening words the man seemed likely to provide. He looked the man over. He was around forty years old, well dressed and had grey hair that he wore slightly long. He had an air of respectability around him that spoke of prosperity.

"Why not? A man gets tired of his own company." Nate rose and offered his vacant table to the young couple, who were very grateful to enjoy the romance of an intimate lunch.

"Paul Tranter, how do you do?"

"Nate Carlton, how do you do?" The two men shook hands, each sizing the other up.

"I must confess that I saw your interlude the other night with the buffalo hunter and admired your restraint. There's many men who would have shot the man dead with less provocation and be done with it. I know you're good enough, by the speed of your draw and how you controlled the situation. You can always tell a good man by their actions of restraint rather than the gun handy kids out to make a name for themselves. They're the ones who'll wind up in an early grave."

"Well, I'm not sure about that," Nate retorted modestly. "I just wanted an end with the minimum of fuss and get out unscathed."

"That's as maybe. Shall we look at the menu, and I'll buy you that drink I promised you?" With the food decided upon, Tranter continued. "I'll declare now that I have an interest in cattle and saw you with those two young punchers. Are you an owner, a rancher yourself? You have the look about you."

Normally such a forward question would have put Nate on edge, but he decided that Tranter had said it in such a way as not to give offence, and he reminded him a little of his father both in his demeanor and his manners. He smiled in reply. "No, sir, I am not. I'll maybe be a rancher someday, but for now I have no real direction other than a desire to see the land further west in Texas."

"In that case we may yet do some business together. I am a cattle buyer and have interests back east. There is a huge demand for beef in the north. They say there's a change coming and that things will open up again. The railroad is moving from the south and one day it'll link to the north, maybe even the west. It'll create new opportunities and growth. This country has suffered enough, and now we need to rebuild. Cattle will be the way and they'll be the new currency of the west, just you mark my words."

"You're sounding pretty evangelical about that," Nate replied. "But as it is, I happen to agree with you. I am going to try my hand at rounding up cattle and see how it goes. I'm going down to San Antonio and join up with a man that the boys were talking about. A man named David Randall, who owns the DR Connected. Have you heard of him?"

"I have, and about his plans to drive a large herd north for the eastern market. He's a hard man, mind, takes no prisoners and he'll ride roughshod over anyone or anything that gets in his way. It'll be a tough school that you'll enroll in under him, of that I'm in no doubt. You'll learn a lot but I've a feeling that so will he. The routes north are largely unmapped and many an ambitious man has lost everything along the way."

"So I hear from the other two. But I haven't much to lose, so as far as I can see I can only gain from the experience."

"I'm sure that you will profit, you have that look and feel about you, and I'm a good judge of men and their worth. It has been my business as much as cattle. Here's my card," Tranter said, fishing into his vest pocket. "You can always reach me via the telegraph office here. Everyone knows me."

Nate took the card and stored it away. They passed the next hour covering all topics from books they'd read to the western states, England—which Tranter had visited—and the opportunities that would come when the railroad opened up the country. Nate enjoyed himself immensely and promised to return the favor the next day, when they agreed once more to meet for lunch. For two more days he shared lunch with Paul Tranter and enjoyed his company. He learned that they were planning to drive the railroad north with a continuation of the Houston and Central Texas Railroad to make Dallas a hub and a major terminus.

Each day he rode out to see something of the country around the town and learn what he could about the terrain and nearby homesteads. He left at different times of day and in different directions, ever wary of the buffalo hunters who might spot a routine and want revenge. He collected his boots from the leather worker and spent a day breaking them in before buying some supplies and preparing for a clandestine departure.

During that time he'd seen Caz again once or twice, when she wasn't being closely chaperoned by the ever present Brad Dexter, who seemed to have some sort of proprietorial claim upon her. Without his presence she was vivacious and sparkling company, but once he arrived, she was always more guarded, and the lights of her personality seemed to dim a little. Dexter did nothing outwardly but there was a hint of menace in his presence, an unspoken threat which was palpable yet somehow indefinable, as though she were cowed by his passive threat. Nate mused on this as he made preparations to leave. It was none of his business, he thought, yet there was a mutual attraction there, of that he was certain. But what did he have to offer any woman? He was drifter, and although he had some coin in the bank he had yet to make his mark or achieve anything of substance. Yet he knew he'd like to meet her again under more auspicious circumstances.

That evening he prepared his horses with a good feed of grain, and at midnight, having settled his bill at the hotel, he slipped quietly out of the back room window, climbed over the veranda and dropped to the alley below. Collecting his saddlebags he moved off quietly to the livery barn and saddled up his two horses, walking them out of a side street into the night. It would be morning before he was missed, and he aimed to put some miles between himself and Dallas in that time.

The railroad south of the town had been completed a few miles down the road and he caught a train at daybreak at one of the stations. He loaded Buck and Patch and headed south towards Austin. There he would feel safe from a sniper's Sharps and could ride on toward San Antonio.

Leaving the train at Austin, he moved to explore the state capital. It was a fine town, with elegant buildings and wide streets that were full of bustle. Commerce seemed to be thriving everywhere. The mighty Colorado River cut down by one side of the town, which covered hundreds of acres, Nate was to find. If he had not decided that he would travel to San Antonio, he knew that he could easily settle here. It was an exciting city, and the Texans were a friendly bunch intent upon culture and prosperity. Divorced from the day to day vagaries of the war and closer to the ports in the Gulf of Mexico the town was growing at a rapid rate, determined to recover from the fighting despite the presence of Union troops that were there supposedly to keep law and order.

Nate knew he needed to move and get settled by the start of winter, and after the conversation with Paul Tranter a plan had started to form in his mind. He bought more supplies, including a branding iron which he had a blacksmith form into the initials NSC wrapped into a single image that was identical to the signet ring on his little finger.

As he traveled west, he encountered a wild country of scrub, grass, soaring sandstone mesas and escarpments interposed with the rivers and lakes providing life-giving water to the grassy plains. More importantly to Nate, it was completely different to South Carolina and the place he'd once called home. This was a wild and untamed land full of promise and adventure. Cattle roamed among the scrub, unbranded and wild, with huge spreads of horns both dangerous and beautiful. He estimated that he was some fifty miles from the ranch from the directions he had been given at the last settlement, and he settled by a small creek.

Behind it there was a natural canyon of sandstone filled with scrub and rich grass, fed by a trickling brook. A mesa rose steeply above it to a high plateau that formed a natural break in the landscape. Trees grew in small copses, offering shade and protection from the weather. He found a cave eroded into the sandstone where he made a comfortable camp, and with some brush he formed a natural barrier that would help keep it dry and warm if the weather turned. Then he set about with an axe, cutting down a few small pines. Trimming them off, he made a barrier to the canyon and had himself a natural corral, supported by a stream and lush grass. He made a funnel of rough posts and rails that led into a holding area with a moving gate to the main canyon.

"Now all we need to do is catch us some cattle," he mused, speaking softly to his two horses. Building a campfire away to the side he set the branding iron to heat and went off to find some.

The first time he tried roping for real he was nearly gored to death by a vicious steer. Only Buck kicking out at the last minute saved him from a painful and ignominious death. The steer caught the kick straight in the head and was stunned for a moment, and whilst he was semi-conscious Nate lassoed him, and this time Buck pulled back as he dismounted, keeping the rope taut.

He pulled the animal to his fire, where he branded his first cow. That done, he herded it into the pen and from there to the canyon. It was clumsily done, he admitted, but before long he had his own brands on some of the cattle. Twice more he made short journeys, now herding two or three back to the pen, roping them, dropping them to the ground and branding them. It was hard, backbreaking work and very dangerous, but he was learning. Twice he was nearly trampled to death, suffering bruises and a sprained wrist, but he survived and learned how to read the cattle. With Buck tired he tried Patch who seemed to have some cow in him, as the two Texans would have said. Patch would immediately lurch in the direction in which the cows were trying to escape. He seemed to enjoy the work, bullying and intimating the cattle as he worked.

For three days Nate worked hard, then took a brief rest to help the horses cool off. In the canyon he found himself looking at a herd of nearly a hundred head of cattle, with some younger calves and an older steer which was already bossing the herd and taking control. Nate was tired, dirty and in need of a cold beer. He decided that as he had no experience of herding cattle other than in twos or threes this would be as much as he could handle for what he wanted. The following day he would push them on a drive to David Randall's DR Connected ranch.

Chapter Fourteen

In the morning he saddled up Patch, knowing that Buck would follow come what may, and started to haze the cattle from the canyon. He pushed the bossy steer with the white blaze to the front and with him moving steadily outward he drove the back of the herd to the entrance. With them all boxed in closely he lassoed the final post, pulling it free, and began pushing them through the gap. The lead steer headed south along an obvious trail through the brush and the others followed him. Everything went to plan. The white blazed steer was a natural leader and as long as he kept going in the right direction all would be well, Nate reasoned. How he would cope at night or the next day he didn't know, but he needed to find out, and if nothing else he would learn by his mistakes, however disheartening they may be.

He made a few basic errors, pushing too fast, not paying attention, losing two or three cattle and having to break off and catch them. He was making about three or four miles an hour at most, and it was hard and dusty work. By mid-afternoon he was dog tired and more by luck than judgement the herd found a creek which the white blazed steer headed for. Nate was content to let him do so. The cattle stopped, and rather than push on he let them rest there. He made a campfire, ate a hasty meal by the water, and with the cattle tired and settled he put in half an hour of gun practice. The Road Agent's Spin was now as smooth as could be, he was pleased to see. His draw was something that happened without thought, and he was even faster now than when he had shot Tyler in the saloon. He had practiced spinning and drawing but did not shoot for fear of disturbing the cattle. That done, he fell asleep almost as soon as he laid his head against the saddle he was using for a pillow, never remembering a time when he'd been more exhausted. He woke with the dawn in a covering of dew that made him shiver inside his bedroll. The nights were now nearly freezing with the onset of November, and he knew the early frosts would come soon.

He rolled up his suggan, shook his boots before stamping his feet into them and went to the stream, where he drank a cup of water. Stark sunlight filtered through the dawn, promising another fine day. He brewed some water, ate some hard tack for breakfast and went to unhobble the horses. For three days he continued in this manner and finally at the end of the last day he saw two riders approaching at a steady lope. He recognized Billy Jo as one of them as he took off his hat and waved in salute from a few hundred yards away, calling as he went.

He slid to a halt within a few feet of Nate. "Nate Carlton, I do declare if that don't beat all. You've become a cow puncher, less'n somebody rounded these up and gave 'em to y'all."

"Let me introduce to my roundup crew, this is Robert E Lee," Nate replied, indicating the white blazed steer, "and those are Stonewall Jackson and Jeb Stewart." He pointed at two others.

"Hah, you old dog. This here is Tim, he rides for the DR, too. Tim, this is Nate, the fella me and Frank was tellin' you about. Don't hold it against him, but he hails from England and South Carolina so there ain't no real hope for him." Tim was an open faced man about the same age as Nate and offered him an easy smile by way of greeting. Billy Jo continued: "But he sure has got a pretty pair of Texas boots."

"They fit like a glove, and I thank you for them. I certainly feel the part even if I'm not Texan. Where's Frank? How is he?"

"He's fine. Say, come on, we'll help you with your herd and get you up onto the ranch proper. We're putting together a huge herd for the drive. Lots of small ranchers and such are all adding to it. Gonna be about three thousand head or more time we're finished."

They caught up on everything, with Billy Jo asking how he got out of Dallas unscathed and Tim wanting to know about the incident.

"Did you see any more of that Caz girl? She sure was pretty. Had a mighty fine voice too."

"I did, but her keeper wouldn't let her off the leash much. Seemed mighty funny to me, but you never can tell."

"Oh, the swish that owned the saloon. Didn't like the look of him," Billy Jo commented.

Tim wanted to know more, and Nate was keen to keep gunplay out of the conversation, knowing how vocal Billy Jo could be when he got excited about something. "Yea, old Nate sure discouraged that hunter, ended up kicking him where man didn't ought to be kicked, and he lost all interest in fighting after that. His friends didn't seem that interested, either."

"Did you take them all on?" Tim asked, wondering if there was more to this man than it seemed.

"Naw, he pulled a gun on them while they was gawpin' at their friend," Billy Jo replied before Nate could. "Should've seen the look on their faces. Say, have you still got that little bitty gun and shoulder holster?" he asked Nate.

"I have indeed." Nate smiled. "But it's too fierce to carry around you Texas boys, you might piss your pants and run off scared to death," he mocked, hoping to draw the conversation away from any serious talk about gunplay.

They jeered at his comment and the discussion turned to other things, much to Nate's relief.

They drove Nate's small herd across the country at a faster pace, given the other two men's experience, heading south toward the DR Connected ranch house. Topping a rise, the cattle smelled water and started moving more quickly. Below them was a large natural lake fed by a small river that meandered through the lee of two small buttes to emerge between the treelined pool. It was a lovely sight. The ranch house was a few hundred feet behind it, on slightly elevated ground. It was built of sawn logs for much of the lower parts, with some stone walling. The upper rooms were laid out well and had small balconies from which you could see out across much of the ranch, Nate guessed. It was a fine building which looked like it had been added to as the ranch prospered.

There were neat outbuildings surrounding the house which gave cover by virtue of the angles, and the whole ranch could be turned into a position of defense if the need arose. It was a clever design, and it was evident that a lot of thought had gone into it. A well had been sunk and was powered by a windmill that fed troughs for the corrals and the house. The whole spread looked well cared for and mature, with plantings of trees for shade and shrubs. It was the sort of thing his mother would have overseen, he realized, the thought coming unbidden. With such feelings came sadness knowing that he would never see her again or listen to her words of wisdom on all matters. He thrust the memories to the back of his mind, not wishing to seem exposed or have his thoughts guessed.

Taking advantage of the fresh grass and water, the cattle milled around the lake and the three men rode up to the house, leaving them to graze.

As they approached, a man of medium build came from the house and stood on the steps to watch them come. He was stocky with broad shoulders and appeared to be in his mid-forties. He was dressed like a rancher, with a leather vest secured by a tie thong as it stretched around the beginnings of a paunch at his stomach. He looked into Nate's eyes, tough and supremely confident in himself, knowing that those around him would always obey his orders. His was a commanding presence but one tempered with a certain arrogance and authority. Nate knew who he was immediately, but Billy Jo introduced him just the same.

"Mr. Randall, this here is Nate Carlton, I mentioned him before and we just met up with him on the range."

"How do you do?" Nate offered.

"Fine, son, fine. Step down." The voice was gravelly and carried authority.

Nate stepped from Patch and shook hands with the rancher, feeling the power in the dry grip.

Randall screwed up his eyes in appraisal. "Fine piece of horseflesh you got there, Carlton. You come far?"

"Yes, sir, from over in South Carolina. I met up with Billy Jo and Frank on the Mississippi by Greenville and they suggested I come here. Told me you might be hiring."

Randall nodded. "We sure are. Cowpuncher's wages are thirty a month and found. I see that you brought some cattle with you. How many head?"

"Well, I tally about ninety-five. Billy Jo said that you were doing a big municipal drive up north to sell to the East."

"I am. Taking up anybody locally that wants to join in and aiming to push a big herd up. Safety in numbers and we'll get a better price if we can command the market. There's a huge shortage of beef now the war's over, and them damn Yankees still gotta eat, so we may as well take their gold that way, rather than fighting them for it." Randall's weathered face creased in a grin.

"Amen to that," Nate replied. "Your terms are fine and I'd be delighted to join you."

"It'll be tough work with little rest once we get the herd moving, so go get yourself settled in and get to know the boys and the range. We're bringing the stock in closer to the home ranges to keep an eye on them with the worst of the winter weather coming on. Move your cattle down to the lower forty. Billy Jo will show you where that's at and then find yourself a bunk and introduce yourself to my foreman, Ted Lineman. He'll tell you the rules and answer any questions you might have. I'll write you out a tally sheet for your stock and run them with mine. There's already one or two different brands out there.

"Now if you'll excuse me, I have some bookkeeping to do, which is the one thing about this whole business I hate and will likely turn me mean and ornery, so best I go inside." This was delivered with a wry grin as he shook Nate's hand again and pushed open the front door to the ranch house.

"Well, Nate, looks like you're one of the crew," Billy Jo enthused. "Let's get your cattle settled, find you a bunk and I'll introduce you to Ted."

With the cattle pushed out onto the range and left there to mix with the DR Connected stock, Nate returned to the ranch and the bunkhouse. A lean, tall puncher was washing his hands in a bowl on the veranda as the day was ending. The other hands were drifting in from the range in twos and threes, tired after a long day's work.

Shaking his hands dry, the man looked up to see Nate and Billy Jo. His face was brown with the sun, and the lines around his eyes were hard. The man looked as tough as old leather, with a strength born of hard work and difficult conditions. There would be no give in him, Nate knew. He'd seen many non-coms in the army who were of a similar disposition. The foreman brushed his hands through his hair and stood upright an inch or two taller than Nate.

"Ted, this is our new hand, Nate Carlton," Billy Jo said. "He fought with your troop in the 4th Virginia Cavalry Regiment."

Ted studied him. "Really? Looks a mite young to me. Which troop?"

"Hanover Light Dragoons, under lieutenant Blackwell. And, yes, I'm just eighteen. Joined up underage."

"A good outfit. Your boys did well, and you came away alive, which is the main thing." The foreman shook hands with Nate, and they moved inside to find a bunk for him. With that done they washed up just as the cook rang the iron for supper.

Nate reflected that it had been easier than he thought and marveled how the little coincidences had helped him. From meeting Sam he'd gone on to partner up with Billy Jo and Frank, which would not have happened without the robbery outside Greenville. On such matters the cards of fate turned, but he remembered his earlier thoughts of his mother, and vowed that one day, when he wasn't protected by the law—such as it was—he would hunt down and kill Craw Gillett to avenge his parents' death. The letter he'd taken from his father's safe was in his money belt. His father's words were still raw to him, and he pushed them from his mind as they gave him a bitter reminder of the family he had lost.

Chapter Fifteen

The weeks turned into months, with the air getting colder as winter came on and the days merging into one in a sea of hard work. Nate helped the rest of the crew riding the range, mending fences, brush popping and herding the cattle down to lower and more protected pastures as the weather became harsher.

He forged friendships with many of the hands. His easy-going nature made him popular and being acquainted with Billy Jo and Frank helped, but there was still an innate reserve within him, a sadness that still crept up upon him from time to time and a promise he'd made to himself that he would one day settle the score for his parents. Despite the company of a friendly bunch of cowboys, he still felt alone in the world at times, and lacked the sense of belonging that had been present in the war when his family had been alive.

Luckily the other two punchers hadn't bragged about his skill with a gun, and he was able to keep up his practice out of sight when he rode the range by himself. It wasn't as much as he would like, but it was enough to keep his speed, hand and eye in line with what he wanted. A few had commented upon the unusual and to them fancy nature of his gun rig, but he played it down and just said that it felt more comfortable. Every one of them carried a gun. They shot with pistols and rifles, using them as tools, and no one bragged about how good or bad they were. Some reckoned that Ted was good with a gun, but little more was said on the matter. The fact that Nate carried two guns, one in a cross draw holster, was cause for more comment, and it marked him as a man who was either trying to make a statement or was really skilled. He deflected the comments, telling anyone who asked that he liked it for when he was riding and it gave him good access for shooting snakes.

It was when spring arrived that all this changed. New hands were drifting in to make up the numbers for the big push north once the weather finally broke and the new grass made trailing a possibility. Some of the older men wanted to stay at home with families and the word got out that the DR Connected was hiring. Three new men arrived in one week. Two were already known to the crew, the third was a hard-eyed man who seemed somehow familiar to Nate, although he could not place him. He was lean and had a cautious look about him. He proved to be a good hand with cattle, but always wore his gun tied down.

"This here is Saul, Rich and Brian," Ted Lineman said. "Three new hands for the trail."

The man he'd introduced as Brian looked around him, as if silently sizing each man up, but said little other than nodding howdy to the group of hands.

The next day as they were riding one of the final swathes of country looking for strays, Nate asked Billy Jo a question. "Do you know that feller Brian? He seems familiar and he looks pretty mean."

"Nope. Never seen him afore. I'll ask around and let you know. Why you askin'? You figure he might be tracking you from Greenville?"

"I just want to know. It's a feeling, nothing more. Could be I'm jumping at shadows."

"Yeah, forget it. Hey, are you still practicing with your gun and drawing? Frank and I were talking about it on Saturday when we went to town."

"Billy Jo, you promised. Did anyone hear you?"

Bill Jo waved him off. "Don't go worryin' yourself. Ain't no one here gonna talk or challenge you to a gunfight. Ted'll fire anyone causes that kinda trouble. I seen him do it, too. Anyways, no one heard far as I'm aware."

"Well, yes. I still practice—but quietly, when I'm out on the range."

"Can you do that twist and fire trick we practiced on the trail?"

Nate shook his head, smiling despite himself. Billy Jo was like a coon hound with the scent of cougar. "Yes, I can. You got me when you thought that one up."

"Ha, I knew it, I just knew it. C'mon, show me."

At which he pointed to a small stream where some fallen cedar elms had blown down. A couple of slender branches now stood perpendicular to the ground set about six feet apart.

"Billy Jo, I swear you're like a kid in a store after candy."

"Oh, come on, it's time for a coffee, anyways. No one around. We've caught all the cattle we can. There ain't no more brush to pop, let's have some fun, just for the hell of it. What do you say?"

The shade under the trees looked cool. It was time for a coffee and the work was done. Also Nate felt the lure of the challenge under pressure. He could turn and spin and shoot all right, but was he faster and more accurate than before? Part of him —the competitive part—wanted to know.

"What the hell, come on then." They made a fire and put the coffee pot on to boil, then made ready. "So how do we do this?" Nate asked.

"Okay, see those two branches stickin' up, one on the left and right? Well you take the left and me the right. I'll face it, you turn away like before. Now..." He picked up a small rock as they dismounted while Nate tied down his holster. "I'll throw this up to the side, and soon as we hear it hit the ground we'll draw. Agreed?"

"Sure, why not?"

The two men took up their positions some thirty-five feet from the fallen tree. Nate, facing away, slipped the thong off the hammer of his Colt. He was nervous but he found himself looking forward to the test.

"Ready?"

"Yep."

"I'm gonna toss it...now!" Billy Jo threw the rock up and to the side so it would land on some shale nearby that was just out of Nate's eyeline. To the two men it seemed like minutes, but it was just a couple of seconds, then the crack came as the rock hit the ground. Both men reacted fast, hands moving in a blur of speed. Nate slipped his gun, drawing as he turned with no conscious thought. Spinning to focus on the target two shots rang out before he had even realized he'd pulled the trigger, severing the branch. A fraction later a third shot echoed across the plain, and a patch of white appeared on the right hand branch as Billy Jo's bullet nicked it.

Billy Jo looked over incredulously as Nate began to rise from a semi crouch, dropping the hammer and pinwheeling the Colt on his trigger finger.

"I don't believe it. I see'd it but I still don't believe it. And I had the edge from throwing the rock. Man, I declare you're faster than ever!"

Nate was secretly pleased. He knew he'd been fast, but even by his standards that display was exceptional. He palmed the Colt and began to reload, setting it to half cock, pushing out the caps, and retrieving the block of paper cartridges from his saddlebag. He rammed home the new balls onto the cartridge, set the nipples and was ready to go. His hands moved with great dexterity, and he knew he could do it in the dark the way Sam had instructed him: *Some owl hoot ain't goin' to wait until sunup to shoot you and you might need to re-load in the dark, so best try now when there ain't no one shootin' back at you.* As with all Sam's wisdom, it made sense, and he had practiced.

"Damn it, Nate, you shaved me off the twist. No one'd ever believe it if they hadn't seen it."

"Let's just keep it that way, can we?" Nate asked, knowing his friend's enthusiasm was matched only by his garrulousness.

"Don't worry, Nate, you got my word. Sure is a shame, though." At that moment hoofbeats were heard and across the hill came two riders. "Looks like Ted and that new man Brian you were asking about," Billy Jo remarked. "We'll just say that we saw a rattler."

"Agreed."

The two men trotted to a halt. "You boys alright? We heard shooting," Lineman asked.

"We saw a rattler. Don't worry, Nate got 'im." Billy Jo jerked a thumb in Nate's direction just as he was putting a new percussion cap on the chamber.

Ted raised an eyebrow, not fooled for a minute.

"Coffee's on the boil, happen you want some," Billy Jo offered.

The two men dismounted at the offer. No cowpuncher refused coffee. Leaving their horses to drink by the stream, they returned with enameled mugs at the ready. Lineman looked over at the fallen tree, saw the fresh mark where the bark had been stripped away, but let the matter drop. The newcomer Brian looked around suspiciously, casting a hard glance at Nate.

"Looks like you shot yourself a tree, not a rattler," he muttered to Nate, peering over his steaming coffee cup.

"Well, we got it in the end, or at least seemed to. The tree was pretty upset, mind you." Nate deflected Brian's hard stare with a smile, refusing to be drawn.

They changed the subject, brooking no further discussion about gunplay. Their coffee finished, each pair went their separate ways looking for more cattle roaming wild to brand and push in towards the ranges closer to the ranch house. Turning back by some instinct, Nate had looked over his shoulder to see Brian giving him another hard stare as he left. Something was off there, but he had no idea what he'd done to offend the man and as far as he was aware. He still looked familiar, but Nate couldn't work out if or where he'd met him before.

The next few days passed as the cattle were gradually being bunched onto the land in the proximity of the ranch house. A chuck wagon and cook named Charlie Bannerman together with his louse Obadiah, a tall thin negro who Charlie swore could see in the dark better than any horse, had been found for the drive. One would drive the chuck wagon, the other the bedroll wagon. These would be the hands' only permanent fixtures for the long drive north. The sourdough keg was fermenting away, and all supplies were being carefully stored and laid ready to load up for the cattle drive. Extra horses had been broken by the wranglers, of which there would be three for the drive, a couple of tow-headed youngsters and a lead wrangler with experience called Steve Jones. He was popular with the men and was acknowledged as someone who could ride anything with hair. He loved his horses and unlike many bronc busters he cared for the animals and was gentle. Woe betide any man who was found mistreating his charges.

The lead wrangler had a way about him, even with the wild ones, and they came up to him naturally. It was a gift that he used well. Nate took to the man and was keen to learn as much as possible from him, picking up little tips and tricks along the trail. They developed a sense of mutual respect, and as Nate leant over the corral watching him break in one of the final mounts for the remuda, he saw him side-pass the line back dun he was riding to end up parallel to the corral rails as though it was the most natural thing in the world with no outward sign of how he had done it.

"Fine riding, Steve," Nate called. "How's that done? Couldn't see how you did it."

Steve grinned down at him, looking younger than his thirty odd years: "Waal now, you sort of drop your weight into the left seat bone, like so," he drawled, exaggerating the movement. "Then you open your hips to encourage him to go where there's space and then push on off, on off, with your lower leg."

He had turned the dun away from the rails giving him the room to move, and sure enough he obediently moved away from the pressure of Steve's left leg, albeit a little awkwardly at first.

"Lovely work. I'll give it a try on Patch. He's coming along nicely but that lateral work is something else. I like a horse that moves away from the leg with ease."

"I seen you ridin' him. That's a fine Appaloosa you have yourself there. Train him yourself?"

Nate nodded.

"Say, um..." Steve continued, suddenly embarrassed. "Waal, Frank mentioned that you helped him and Billy Jo with his letters and such. The thing is I can't read or write none and we're all gonna be thrown together a lot on the drive. I sorta wondered if maybe you could help me, too?"

"Sure, Steve, I'd be glad to." There was so much thirst for knowledge out here, Nate realized. Everyone seemed to want to improve their lot. They weren't stupid, he knew that much. They just never got the opportunity to learn.

"The thing is, I don't want to be a wrangler all my life, I'd like to make something of myself and get me some book learning. A man's no good if'n he can't read what's writ on the page and sign his name and do figures and such. I'd appreciate it, Nate.

"Billy Jo also told me..." Steve looked around furtively, making sure no one was within hearing distance. "...that you're pretty good with that." He nodded down at Nate's waist and his six gun. "Now don't worry none, he said it quiet like. I'm just curious, 'cause we might just have ourselves some trouble brewing. That new hand Brian's been askin' questions about you and he seems to me like a bad horse. He's lookin' for trouble, if you know what I mean. He has a bad eye, that one. I see it in horses and I see it in men. Anyway, watch yourself. Now I need to get back to it."

At which he pushed the dun into a lope around the outside of the corral, stopping him by his seat, spinning him around through a one eighty turn and pushing off on the other lead.

Damn it, Nate thought, *trouble follows me wherever I go.* He wondered once again what it was with Brian. He thought no more of it as the cook rang for supper time and all the hands swarmed towards the bunkhouse, gathering for their food. They were hungry and dived in to feed themselves after a hard day's work.

Brian was at the other end of the long table and met his eye once with a hard stare. Nate ignored him and started to clean up his plate, then suddenly he wasn't hungry. A tension was building in him. Some instinct told him that a conflict was coming, and he couldn't face a whole trail drive not knowing when it might all explode in his face. He picked up his plate of half-eaten food, rose and went to dump it in the wash bowl.

"Not hungry, Nate?" Billy Jo called to him.

"Naw, I ate something that didn't agree with me—probably your cooking," he joked with a smile and stepped outside before anymore comments could follow.

"Goddamn easterner ain't got the stomach for anythin'." He heard the muttered comment as he left. He couldn't identify the speaker, but it didn't take too much guesswork. Nate didn't often smoke, but he pulled a small cigar from his pocket, struck a match and felt the rush of tobacco settle him. Maybe he was imagining it. Was it all in his mind? Yet Steve had warned him there was trouble brewing. *Trust your instincts.* Remembering Sam's warning months before, he bent and tied the cord around his leg.

That done he decided to go and practice. He stepped off the veranda and into the sunlight that was now casting long shadows as evening drew in. He squinted his eyes against the light and the tobacco smoke that drifted up past his face. Maybe he should move on, but he also knew it was against his nature to avoid trouble. Maybe he should just face Brian down and ask him what was bothering him.

The decision was taken out of his hands when he heard the door open and steps on the veranda behind him: "What's the matter, ain't you got no stomach for anything? Seems to me you got a yaller streak goin' right through you."

Nate recognized Brian's voice.

Other steps were now heard upon the wood as more of the hands left the table to see what was happening, all of them sensing trouble.

Nate ignored him, taking the last puff on his cheroot before grinding the butt under his heel.

"What's the matter? Afraid to turn around?" Brian taunted him. "Or can you only shoot people when they ain't facing you?"

Nate frowned and turned back to face the bunkhouse. "What the hell are you talking about?" he said. "You've been giving me the eye since you arrived. Do I know you? Have I done something to offend you? Because I would certainly like to know what it might be."

The ranch hands fanned out now, sensing a shooting, getting out of the line of fire. Like Nate, Brian had his gun belt on.

"You forget so easy? My name is Brian Wallace, and you killed my brother Chord headin' down to Greenville on a riverboat. Remember?"

"I remember. He was in a set up laying for a friend of mine. He was going to shoot him because his partner was cheating at cards. It was all settled by the captain of the boat. Witnesses saw it and agreed. I gave him every chance, but he was going to kill my friend. Now, can't we just leave it be, I don't want any trouble." Nate felt the anger building in him, but he wanted to stay on here and he knew that if he drew he would kill this man, and another death would be on his conscience. Ted had warned him about fighting, and he was beginning to like this ranch and looking forward to the trail ahead. He also knew with absolute certainty that he would win. At which he turned his back and began to walk away, hoping to avoid another killing.

"You're a liar. You shot Chord in the back! Just like I shot your friend Sam Kennedy in the back. I killed him stone dead, and now I'm gonna kill you, too." The words stopped Nate in his tracks. Had this man really killed Sam or was he winding him up for action? It was taken out of his hands. "Now face me, coward—draw!"

The words overrode all conscious thought on Nate's behalf. His hand flew to the Navy Colt and he dropped, span and fired in one fluid blur of movement. Two bullets hit Wallace just as his gun was clearing the leather and a look of pure surprise came over his face. He tried to raise his gun as he staggered backward under the impact of the two slugs. But his arm was heavy and despite a final effort of will he was unable to lift it. Instead, he fell forward, dead before he hit the boards outside the bunkhouse. There was a stunned silence as Nate rose from his crouch, gun ready in case of any further trouble.

One of the young hands, Jack, whistled: "Man, oh man, did you see that? He barely cleared the leather and he had the drop on you. I ain't never seen anything like it."

With the exception of Billy Jo and Frank, the rest of them were just as amazed. They had known Nate as a hard-working and friendly young puncher who never boasted or bragged, a reserved young man who kept himself to himself. Now they would talk, and no one would keep a lid on this incident. Now he would have to move on.

"Someone get a shovel or two. He'll need burying," Ted Lineman ordered. He'd seen such corpse and cartridge affairs before and would again, he assumed. Then turning to Nate he said: "It was a fair fight, Nate, you've got nothin' to worry about. We're all friends here and you did everything you could to avoid trouble."

Nate nodded his head in acknowledgement of Ted's words. The man was fair and he would treat Nate no differently after this—other than maybe offering him a little more respect.

"I wonder if he really did kill Sam Kennedy," Ted continued. "Can't see someone like this gettin' the drop on a man like Kennedy. He a friend of yours?"

Nate looked away from the sight of the dead gunman. "Sam? Yes he is, and I hope he is still alive. When he said he'd killed Sam I assumed he was telling the truth. I don't know anyone who could pull down on Sam face to face in a fair fight and live to boast about it."

"I can think of one, and that's you. That was the fastest draw I've ever seen. But we'll keep quiet about that and like I say, you're welcome to stay on for the drive. Give you a chance to drift and get lost. Which is something you'll probably want, unless you want a rep with young kids coming after you lookin' for a notch in their guns.

"When we hit Abilene, you can go your own way and just disappear. The west is a big country. But one thing's for sure. Word'll get around if you stay here, and someone will come huntin' you someday. I'm sorry but we can't have that. Mr. Randall will let you stay and be part of the drive. I'll square it away with him when he gets back from town, but after that he'll want you gone, I'm afraid."

It was a finite statement, but it was better than Nate had hoped for. He nodded.

"Sure, Ted, I understand and appreciate the effort on your behalf. I'll be away when the drive's done," Nate assured him.

Nate wandered off into the evening to lose himself in his thoughts. He felt sick. It was another killing he did not want. He wanted peace after the war, and the anger that had boiled within him after learning of his parents' death had cooled to an icy feeling of revenge that he would take in due course. But his feeling towards his fellow man had become more temperate. He wanted a peaceful life and the chance to move on and make something of himself. He sighed and shook his head, realizing that all Sam's teaching had paid off and without it, it would be him lying back there outside the bunkhouse waiting to be buried. His gun had just appeared in his hand, muscle memory driving him to turn and crouch, the hammer slipping without him even remembering it happening.

Then he thought about Sam.

He'd heard nothing on the prairie telegraph and it had been months since they'd parted company. Surely someone would have set the rumors flying if one of the most notorious gunmen in Texas had been killed, even hundreds of miles away to the east. He made up his mind to telegraph the sheriff's office in New Orleans when he got the chance to see if there was any word of a killing.

The darkness was falling, and it was getting cold as the spring air had not warmed up enough to keep the evenings pleasant. He felt alone again and empty. Another killing,

Sam possibly dead, and now he was alienated from the ranch crew with a notice upon his head to quit once the herd was delivered. Nowhere to call home, he had no family that he knew of apart from a brother many thousands of miles away who he hadn't seen for years. This was not what he'd anticipated when the war finished. He had wanted peace and a return to normal life. He had no trade, and no skill that he could use to make a living except the ability to use a gun exceptionally well. Then he mentally shook himself. He would finish the drive and learn the skills of cattle driving, and next time he'd put his own herd together. He had capital, there were hundreds of thousands of unbranded wild cattle out there, and the east was starved of beef.

It couldn't be that difficult, he considered, with drive and an ability to learn. He'd learned how to use a gun and rope cattle, and he was sure more skills would come.

Chapter Sixteen

It was a crisp spring morning, and the smell of crushed sagebrush mixed with the tang of thousands of cattle and horses beginning to break into a sweat filled the air as the punchers hazed the cows into a rough line that would form the shape of the journey north in the weeks to come. Spears of gentle red shot across the south Texas skyline as the sun broke from the east and threw long shadows that danced across the hard beaten ground like drunken puppets.

The cattle had been brought up to the line of the main trail some half a mile from the ranch house and held in abeyance overnight by the nighthawks. These were the older crew members who would not make the drive and could be used for this last arduous chore before the trail crew took over.

David Randall rode up, looking fresh and ready for the off. He was there to represent the ranch, and as a figurehead he might do his share, but Ted Lineman was the trail boss, and all would bow to his word. Frank had been appointed as second in command while Steve Jones headed up the remuda with a couple of young wranglers who had made the grade. Charlie sat aboard his chuck wagon with the huge sourdough keg strapped to the side. The cook's louse was the old negro, Obadiah whose creased and seamed face had witnessed more trail drives than any of them and who would support them through thick and thin with a hot meal whatever the weather.

The cattle lowed and bellowed, annoyed at being made to rise so early and forced forward from their comfortable positions near water and fresh grass. Dust was already starting to rise as the huge herd reluctantly began to move, following the lead steers who swung their huge racks of horns to and fro. Already a mean looking old bull of the woods seemed to dominate the others, pushing to the front and challenging any and all to usurp his position with a mean look in his eye. He had huge muscular shoulders and outweighed any of the other stock by a good hundred pounds. His dappled red coat was splashed with white in a distinctive manner.

"Sure is a pretty sight, Nate, ain't it?" Frank nodded at the sprawling herd before them.

"That it is, and one I'll never forget or tire of watching," Nate replied.

Then the time honored cry came roaring across the plain: "Move 'em out, head 'em north. Come on, you worthless saddle tramps, let's get 'em going," Lineman shouted above the noisy scene before them.

"Well, that's how you tell a trail boss," Frank said. "Never happy unless we're all working, and I think that's our call to duty. Yee-ha! Let's go, Nate, we're off to Abilene!" Frank grinned and spurred his horse on.

It was always harder to get reluctant cattle to move off their home ground, Nate was to learn, but gradually the whole line thinned as the magnificent beasts swayed and pushed northwards under a morning sky that was opening up before them. The hands were fully occupied for the first mile as the cattle tried to back out and return home, dodging the ropes and the cutting horses that herded them in tightly, bruising shoulders by barging at just the right angle to unbalance the cow and dissuade it from trying to escape.

In a brief moment of respite after about three miles Nate found himself riding next to Frank again. "We're moving at a hellish pace. Will we ride this fast all the way to Abilene?"

"Naw. Hell, we'll keep this up for the first day or so, get the critters off home ground, tire 'em enough to take the cussedness out of 'em and bed 'em down well. Mebbe do that for the first two or three days and then ease off some, or they'll be nothin' but hide and tallow time we get to Abilene."

Nate nodded, storing the knowledge away for future reference. Then seeing a mother and calf try to dodge out, he nudged his cutting horse forward into a fast lope in the direction of the errant cows. The horse, as part of the ranch remuda, knew its job without being asked. It took just the right line, coming from behind the cow, making contact with its shoulder and avoiding the dangerous looking horns that the beast tried to bring to bear. Nearly losing her balance the mother took the hint and moved back to the herd, her calf sticking to her side and lowing as it went.

Gradually the herd and punchers found a rhythm as each man settled to his work, learning which were the troublemakers, which would keep going and when to break for food in the middle of the day. To Nate's eyes Lineman seemed to be everywhere at once, offering an encouraging word or shouting orders to any slackers and occasionally taking part in cutting and returning cattle. He systematically chose each man to go to the drag and relieve those who had already done their shift there. Nobody liked the drag. It was hard work keeping the stragglers in line, constantly monitoring what was going on, with little vison due to the choking dust. Each man raised and tied his large silk bandana over his face when he was in this position to ward off the worst of the clogged red air. It helped but it never completely blocked the dust that seemed to coat every man's throat as they rode drag. They drank from their canteens as much to spit the dust from their mouths as to slake their thirst.

At the end of the first day with the sun starting to dip into the western sky and dusk creeping in with wild hues of orange and scarlet etching across the deep blue of the darkening light, they halted the herd near a small river. The banks were soon chewed up by hooves of the cattle, exhausted after a fifteen mile push, and after drinking their fill they lay down to chew the cud and sleep. A few members of the first night herd shift came in early, ate their supper and with the cattle seemingly settled went out to sing the herd to sleep. The rest of the crew grabbed their food and settled down to get some sleep before being called out to relieve the early shift. And so another rhythm was set up for the long days ahead upon the trail, a rhythm that would govern their lives until they reached Abilene.

The smell of the hot thick stew made Nate's stomach rumble and his mouth salivate. Walking away from his horse he dropped his saddle on its side. "I do declare," he said, "if there wasn't any food I'd go and eat a raw cow, I'm that damned hungry!"

The others laughed and Frank chimed in: "Sure makes a man hungry herding all them dogies for miles on end. Course, we'n all heard you snoring away under that big sycamore as we passed but we didn't like to disturb you none so we just tiptoed on by."

The others joined in with the ribbing, and for a few moments any thoughts of his tenuous position within the ranch and its crew were forgotten amidst the banter of a group of men he was pleased to call friends. Nate approached the chuckwagon and was handed a huge plate of scalding dark brown stew and some freshly made biscuits and potatoes.

"There you go, son, fill yer up and keep you goin'," the cook offered.

"Thank you, Charlie, but I might be back for more."

Five minutes later he was, and with the meal finished he rolled up in his suggan, dog tired, and was asleep in moments before he was called for night duty in the early hours. It seemed to Nate like it was only a few seconds later when he was roused from a deep sleep. He thanked the puncher who shook him and struggled to get up, unbending his stiff body. Shaking out his boots to check for spiders and scorpions he stamped them on and slid his gun belt around his waist, checking the guns in an action that was now instinctive. He pulled a sheepskin coat about him to ward off the early morning chill and walked over to the remuda that was held in a cable corral.

Each hand had chosen their pick for the drive, and it was Steve Jones' job along with his two assistants to know which man rode which horse for the entire drive. Nate found Buck waiting for him, saddled. He didn't need a cutting horse for night duty and Buck would alert him ahead of any human ears if trouble was abroad. He stepped into the saddle with a creak of leather and moved out slowly to circle the herd, singing to them about the Camptown Races as he went. The cattle were tired after the first day's drive, and he could sense no trouble brewing. Even the muleys that Frank had warned him to watch out for were quiet. They were grouped together off to one side, seemingly content, with none of their horned cousins trying to chase them off.

Nate heard a wolf howl off in the distance, but nothing else untoward happened during his watch. He was alert for signs of trouble, but the first night passed quietly and was grateful for it. He was met by his relief, who had been woken by the nighthawk and came out to take over from him and two other riders who had been circling the herd. Nate rode back to his bedroll, clipped up the tarp and was asleep in seconds.

It seemed like only minutes later that he was woken by the sound of the cook's triangle clanging the hands awake to tell them breakfast was ready and there was work to be done. "Come and get it while it's good and hot, be daylight soon," Charlie shouted.

The camp gradually came to life as men grunted and stretched, easing their aching muscles into life.

The second day of the drive began. The cattle were rousted and driven protesting from their beds and their grazing. Each man took his place, from the point, wings and flank to the dreaded drag. Today it was Nate's turn to take this onerous position, which he accepted with resignation, glad that it had not become too dusty and that the smattering of chewed and trampled grass still held the soil together and kept the dust down.

The herd began to heed the urging of the cowhands and walked northward at an ambling gait. Then through the dust as he had swung out to push back an errant cow he saw up ahead two large fissures in the rock that caused a narrowing of the trail. At one side just before them sat Ted Lineman with his horse held still at ninety degrees to the herd, and about twenty yards away on the other side sat Billy Joe. Nate saw them point and nod at each cow, totally absorbed in what they were doing. The herd had thinned as they were funneled through the naturally occurring gap presented by the break in the rocks, going through no more than four or five at a time, with the flank and swing riders hazing them into line. Watching them in puzzlement, he was jerked from his reverie as one of the other point men shouted to him to come on back and get to work. He shook himself and cantered back to keep the drag moving.

"What's going on, Jim?" he shouted at the puncher next to him.

"They're doin' a head count. They always do it in places

like this. The gap in the rocks there forms a natural gate. Thins out the herd and makes it easier to count 'em."

"No. You're joshing me," Nate replied incredulously.

"No, sir, I ain't." Jim smiled under his bandana. "Count has to be done so's we know how many we got and it can only be done when they're on the move. You'll see soon enough when we get all these critters through the gap."

At which he veered away to push back another cow who was making a break for it. Nate shook his head, but sure enough when the last of the herd passed through the break in the rocks Ted and Billy Jo were still earnestly concentrating on the job of counting every one of them. He saw that they had a piece of rawhide cord in their hands with knots and loops made in it. Periodically they added another loop or knot as more cows went through.

On they went, never stopping, eating the miles away. At supper that night Nate was still curious.

"Billy Jo, tell me how it works, I'm still puzzled," he asked.

"Waal now, you see we got to know how many there are in the herd. We'll likely lose a few, hell we'll prob'ly eat a few too, and along the way some more'll naturally join us. If'n they're branded we'll turn 'em away. If they ain't we'll slap a DR Connected brand on 'em and keep up. Rule of the land. Randall will have purty accurate idea of how many head he owns, so we kinda need to check by doin' a head count, you see?"

"Yes, but how? I saw no pen and paper—just rawhide and string."

"Yup, that's right. See I may not be a real smart limey like you." He grinned back at Nate. And I gotta take my boots off if I have to count past ten!" Nate gave Billy Jo a harsh look, at which he relented. "Okay, okay." He laughed. "We point out the first one and agree on it, and after that we count as we go, putting a knot in the cord every hundred and a loop or some other sign for every thousand. It's simple and we don't have to take our eyes off the herd to do it."

"How accurate is it?"

"Me and Ted was two apart in the total of three thousand two hundred and twenty three head."

"No, really?"

"Honest to God. You go ask Ted what he got," Billy Jo offered.

Expecting a joke and keeping his eye on him so there was no signaling, he asked Ted, who gave the figure two short of Billy Jo's with a wry smile.

"Damn, I have a lot to learn," Nate said shaking his head.

"You're getting there, boy, and learnin' fast. One day you might make a passin' good trail hand," Ted told him, and Nate realized that was high praise indeed from the taciturn trail boss.

Chapter Seventeen

A few weeks later the herd pushed north up through the side of the Texas Panhandle into Oklahoma territory. They waded the Red River and Lineman gave a few head of cattle to the Chickasaw Indians that would allow them to move on peacefully in the direction of Oklahoma City. The herd would bypass the city itself, but they could purchase essential supplies with a couple of hands riding into the town.

As time passed they moved north into the Indian Nation. Here was the time to be wary and more vigilant than ever, Nate had been warned. He had been shadowing the trail scout for the morning after they learned that he had scouted for the army and been taught by the Cherokees serving the old regiment.

The half breed scout Taylor Black Bear who rode for Randall needed a break and had been testing Nate all morning. The man had spoken little but had watched him and asked what he had seen at intervals. Nate related it all as an Indian would, giving details of tracks he had found, water pools, changes in the terrain and signs of unshod ponies off to the west as he traveled right and left across the proposed route of the drive. Nate had been alert and on tenterhooks the whole time, and although he was relieved to be away from the drag and breathe clean air, he found scouting just as taxing, knowing that the fate of the herd fell upon his shoulders and depended on whatever he may or may not see.

He must have done well enough in the eyes of the experienced scout. Taylor grunted and rode off back to the herd, leaving Nate and signaling that he should stay on duty. He had passed another test, he thought to himself, and slowly but surely he was learning how to get by in this raw western world.

He took time to pull off his Stetson, wipe his brow and look at the herd down in the valley below from his vantage point on the escarpment. It was an amazing sight. The herd wended its way across the landscape like some huge primeval monster, shifting and blurring among the dust. He watched stragglers and wayward cattle try to stop and break away from the herd. Nate felt good to be alive, and in that moment he felt a huge sense of exhilaration at what he had become part of.

"Come on then, Patch, let's scout around and make sure they don't all fall down a big hole that I failed to see."

The Appaloosa shook its head up and down in frustration, keen to be off. The young horse eased off smoothly into a working trot, disappearing below the sight line into a mix of scrub and shrubs that clung to the sun bleached crags. Crossing over the ridge carefully so as not to outline himself against the sky, Nate looked down on a plain bisected by a river and a valley of new green grass pushing through with the spring. A herd of buffalo grazed off to the west in the distance, but they would be outside the track of the herd. Even at that distance he caught the rancid smell of the animals, wafted along by the prevailing wind, and raising his eyeglass for a closer look he saw the big shaggy heads nodding and swaying, constantly sniffing the air and watching for danger.

"Sure is a fine sight, Patch," he muttered then looked more closely at the grassy valley trying to pick out a possible campsite for the night. With this done he crossed the trail, heading down into the valley ahead of the herd to assure himself that the land held no traps, no hidden ravines of gullies that would harm the cattle. This done, he headed back in a straight line for the point and spotted Ted Lineman out at the front as usual, his large frame and distinctive style of riding easily distinguishable in the panoply before him.

Nate trotted up, bringing his horse to a firm halt before the trail boss. "Ted," he said. "They seem to be coming along well."

The big man nodded. "They do, they do. What have you got for me?" he asked, sparing no words.

"We crest that rise over yonder." Nate gestured. "Then the land slopes down into a green valley. Buffalo off to the west, quite a way off so they shouldn't trouble us at all. There's a sizeable river but it looks easy enough to cross, not too swollen from the spring thaw, and some stepping off points, then clear as the eye can see it's grass.

"There are tracks of unshod ponies. Small bands, so have your rifle ready. Some shacks, too, settlers again off to the west, maybe a settlement, smallholdings by the look of it, a few clusters of them. I'm surprised they can survive with the Indians so close."

"They do, damned nesters. They stick like shit to a blanket." Ted cursed. "Have to watch 'em, they'll take anything that strays. Worse than Indians thataways. Least they come up and ask for beef or trade. Damned nesters sneak off with a few head and hide 'em away. Need to keep a close watch, the Old Man hates 'em. Some of 'em encroached on his land and tried for a water hole back in Texas, but we dissuaded 'em, and we will here, too, if'n they try to start trouble. Their sheep crop the grass so low it don't grow back." To emphasize the point he spat a wad of chewing tobacco off to the side of his horse.

Nate was surprised at the vehemence in Ted's normally sanguine manner, but he knew that there was history there, and Old Man Randall was a tough, hard man. That much he had seen so far.

"How far's the river?" Ted asked, changing the subject.

"Three, maybe four miles."

"Right, we'll tighten up, I don't want them stampeding when they smell it. We've seen no real water for two days. Ride back and warn the crew, will you? Then get back out there and keep a wary eye."

Nate nodded and gave his old cavalry response in a mock salute: "Yo." He whirled the impatient Patch off to warn the swing and flank of what he had seen. Once done, he headed out to the front again, then off to high ground where he had a good vantage point from which to keep guard. A scout could never do enough, he was coming to learn.

His eyes were not as good as the Indian scout, but he scanned the horizon carefully with his spyglass, picking up every nuance of the terrain and action that passed before him. He was scanning to the west when he saw it: a mother with her two calves had hidden in a wallow, entered along a narrow pass a little further on and had made for an old stream or bed, or toward lush grass, he couldn't make it all out fully. He waited patiently, and sure enough she came out on the other side of a rock fissure a few minutes later, heading away from the herd to what he could only assume was a small valley of green grass beyond. He shook his head at the stubbornness of the cattle, killing themselves by leaving the herd, always thinking they knew best just to get to that extra bit of grass. He noted it and watched the rest of his huge charge as the herd rumbled on towards the river.

As the cattle finally approached the river he saw the crew carefully haze them to almost a standstill, pushing them wide so they would not crowd the crossing and drown the weak steers and the calves. It was skillful work that required patience and constant vigilance. When they were nearly across he rode down off his perch to tell Ted of the escaped mother and calves.

Ted was sat with Randall as he told them, pointing to where they'd headed.

"Them damned nesters will have taken 'em. They'll keep 'em on their range once there." "Old Man Randall snarled. "Round up Bob and Joe, they're handy with their guns. Nate, you can show us where they're at."

"Want me to come, too, sir?" Ted asked.

"No, you stay here and take care of the herd. We'll be

back in a while. Ain't gonna let a few nesters bother us."
With that, he hailed the two punchers called Bob and Joe,
old hands of his from a few years back, both seasoned and
tough men who lived and breathed the brand and
worshipped the old man, Nate knew.

The four men put their legs to their horses and set off in
the direction that the wayward cattle had taken. They soon
reached the wallow, and sure enough an old stream bed with
a trickle of water running through showed evidence of their
passing and the tracks were easy to follow. It was a couple of
miles of easy tracking running through green alfalfa that was
sweet and lush, mixing with the coarser praise grass. The
cattle had moved, grazing as they went, through a cutting
and into a fertile valley that spread out before them to some
of the finest land Nate had ever seen. The small river that the
herd had just crossed meandered through it, and it was
partially protected by rock escarpments on each side.

"They surely are headed to critter paradise! Whoo-ee,"
Joe commented.

"Yeah, and I'm betting we find them by that homestead
yonder." Old Man Randall pointed. Sure enough, as they
rode they saw tracks of a shod horse that had merged with
the cattle and herded them onto the smallholding where they
now grazed on the grass nearby. As they drew closer the door
opened to present a man in his mid-thirties, worn thin with
work and dressed in homespun clothes, a cheap Wolseley hat
sitting askew upon his head.

"Howdy," he called a little warily, a young boy of about
ten years old appearing at his side. The four riders ranged up
in front of the house as their horses slid to a halt.

"Howdy nothin'," Randall said. "Mister, you stole my cattle. I see 'em right there and your horse tracks show you herded 'em in."

"Now you see here, mister. Them cows was roaming free. I didn't see any herd near here, I din't know nothin' about it, and I didn't spot the brand there. Damn it, they wandered in of their own choice. Sure they're here now but there ain't no harm done. I didn't take 'em off you and you can take 'em right back. I sure don't want no trouble and didn't take 'em on purpose." The man was clearly frightened by the presence of the tough looking Connected crew.

"Don't make no never mind," Joe stated flatly. "You got 'em and now we got you dead to rights. Mister you're a cattle thief and you know what we do with cattle thieves."

"No, no. I didn't take 'em, I tell you. Just take 'em back." The man made shooing motions at the cow and her calves, who stepped back a couple of paces and then resumed cropping the lush grass.

"We let you get away with it, then what about all the others?" Randall waved across the valley. "All these other goddamn nesters'll think that the DR Connected's a soft touch. They'll think I can be stolen from and my name'll be worth nothing. You gotta pay the price. Get a rope, Joe."

Joe, who had been carefully building a loop, spurred his horse quickly forward and his lariat flicked out, dropping the loop neatly over the farmer's head.

"Bob, get his horse outta the corral," Randall ordered.

Nate looked on in horror. He knew the law of the land as well as any man, but to see a man hanged over this? It would be a travesty of justice. The man wasn't a rustler, he was just a poor unlucky farmer trying to eke out a living for his family. With him gone his family wouldn't last the summer.

"Mr. Randall," Nate said calmly.

"What?" Randall snapped.

"Look, if I offer to pay for these cattle, you can do a bill of sale and then it will all be legitimate, and you can spare the man his life. What do you say?"

"I say butt out. It ain't none of your business. You've done your job, now let me do mine," he barked.

"But Mr. Randall, he's just a man trying to make a living, and he's got a family. He didn't sneak in and steal the cattle from the herd. They just wandered off. I saw them wander away from the herd and there was no one there to cut them back in. Damn it, it's our fault as much as this man's. Are you really going to see him hang for that?"

"No, he surely ain't!" The door to the house opened and a handsome woman stood there, wisps of blonde hair blowing about her face. In her hands was a shotgun, and as they watched she cocked back the hammers, a sound that echoed in the strained silence that followed. Her dress strained against her lean figure, and the tension was etched across her face. She was nervous but determined, and meant business to save her man, as all could see. Slightly behind her in the shadows stood another girl who was difficult to make out against the shade of the house.

"Ma'am, your husband's a cattle thief and the law's the law. Now put the scatter down afore you get hurt," Randall commanded.

"No, sir, I will not," the woman replied. "Take your damned cattle and begone, but you're gonna leave my husband alone," she stated firmly, her voice betraying the tension in her. She was close to breaking point, all could see, and the scatter was pointed at Randall, the woman's finger whitening against the trigger.

Her husband was mounted on his horse with a rope around his neck and was on the point of being led to a sycamore tree in the yard by Joe.

"I mean it. One more step and I let go, and you'll be first to get it, mister," she threatened Randall.

Everyone knew what a shotgun would do at close range, it could cut a man in half or take Old Man's head clean off.

Out of the corner of his mouth he whispered to Nate. "Ted says you're fast and accurate. Shoot and wound her if need be but break this," he hissed.

"I won't do that, Mr. Randall. I will not shoot a woman," Nate responded, appalled at what he had been asked to do.

With his next words Nate realized the caliber of the man that Randall was. He had sand to burn, he saw.

"Right then, ma'am, you best get to it and shoot me, then your husband will be hung, followed by you, and your children will be orphans, but I mean to take my pound of flesh."

With that Randall moved forward quickly so that his horse was beside the farmer's. Now any buckshot would take them both out. Carefully keeping himself between the woman and her husband he backed up.

Then there was a roar as the shotgun went off and the woman sobbed. She had fired into the air, the report startled everyone, and Nate instinctively went for his gun, staying the movement at the last second. The horse upon which the farmer sat bucked and shied. The only sound was the wife sobbing through her hands as she dropped the gun to the floor. Her daughter's arms were around her, trying to comfort her. The farmer then began to plead as the rope was thrown over the main branch of the sycamore. Then, apparently resigned to his fate he closed his eyes and started to recite the Lord's Prayer, his legs crushing against the flanks of the animal upon which he sat, hoping against hope that he would not be parted and fall to the noose.

At the horse's side Joe stood ready, a rope raised ready to strike the horse on its quarters and send it away, leaving the farmer to dangle by the rope around his neck. He looked across at Old Man Randall, who nodded, and his hand fell. At the same moment that the rope made contact with the horse, a deep shot rang out from a heavy caliber weapon. The horse jumped, and with him came the farmer trailing a loose rope from around his neck.

"What the hell?" Randall cried out.

He turned to see Nate cocking and putting another shell into the breech of the Spencer. In all the confusion and noise he'd been able to slide the rifle from his saddle scabbard, and had cocked and loaded it without anybody watching.

"Now you all just sit tight, and everything will be just fine," Nate said. "Ma'am have you got your husband safely with you?" he shouted over his shoulder as the horse bolted back to its home and the farmer was pulled from it by his grateful wife, who shouted that she had. He also heard horses' hooves in the distance and assumed others from the neighboring steads were coming to see what all the shooting was about. "Good. Get him inside, get your scatter and have it ready and bolt the doors, do you hear me?

"Now, Mister Randall. I am a reasonable man, and I won't see a simple soul killed for a couple of lousy cows. That man is no rustler and you're no hanging judge. Let it be and—Bob, leave it! This Spencer will blow a hole in your boss first, and don't think I still can't drop you and Joe before you pull down on me," Nate said from the off side of his horse.

"Leave it, Bob. You're finished, Carlton, I'll ruin you!" Randall snarled.

"Maybe you will, maybe you won't. It's been tried before and I'm still here. Now I assume by your hostile manner that you won't want me on the drive anymore?"

"Damn right, I won't. You're fired, and if I ever see you again I'll kill you!" he shouted.

"Fair enough. People have said that before, too. But you still owe me for my bill of sale for my ninety five head as per the agreement that we both signed to go on the drive. I'll see you in Abilene for that or you can leave it as a draft at the National Wichita bank. Your choice either way. I'll see the money in Wichita or I'll see you again."

Randall just fumed. "And I'll see you in Hell first," he said.

"That can be arranged. Be warned that I'll come collecting, and hiding behind your tame gunnies here won't help you a bit. Meantime getting a reputation as a welcher and a coward isn't going to help you do business, I'm certain of that."

Randall's hands clenched and Nate thought that he had

pushed him too far. For a moment he thought Randall would rush him despite the gun covering him. Yet he stayed on the spot, apoplectic with rage. No one had faced him down like this in years and he already hated the story that would be told, as he knew it would.

"Right, this is how it will play out," Nate continued. "I am taking your horses with me for a mile, then I'll leave them tied to a bush on the trail we took. That way I'll have enough time to clear the herd and be on my way. You gentlemen will have a short walk and then all will be well with the world."

The three men cursed him as he gathered their mounts up by the reins. "Be nice," he told them, "and I'll make it half a mile. Now, it's been nice working with you gents and I hope there are no hard feelings. I'll leave you your pistols, but I'm taking your long guns. Just drop the belts on the ground and walk away, I don't want to be shot in the back."

The three complied with more cursing and retreated a few yards.

"Much obliged, I would hate to have to shoot you." He smiled at them. "I'll loop them over that tree yonder." He gestured.

With that he picked up the three gun belts, saddled the Spencer, remounted and began to back Patch away from the men, leading the other horses. As he did so, he saw dust in the distance a few hundred yards off from one of the other settlements and knew that the farmer and his family would be safe. He clucked and urged his horse backwards, and after about thirty yards he span him around and set off at a fast canter. A hundred yards on he stopped and looped the three gun belts over a low hanging branch and cantered off towards the herd, leading the three spare horses behind him. He tied them to a hawthorn bush after another five hundred yards. He took off his hat, gave a friendly wave and was off in a cloud of dust.

Behind him the wife of the farmer appeared again, this time with the reloaded shotgun. Her daughter came out behind her carrying an old Dragoon Colt that she held in two hands. In the distance she saw three of her neighbors cantering toward the house and realized she'd soon have the advantage of numbers and knew that all would be well.

"Now, gentlemen, this time it's loaded with buckshot not birdshot and I will shoot you if you bother us again. Take your mangy cattle and git!"

"Birdshot! You mean she warn't even loaded for bear?" Bob exclaimed.

Randall was silent and morose, but Bob laughed without mirth. "Well, ma'am, I do admire your gall, I surely do," he said. "We won't hurt you none. We got other fish to fry, and that there Nate surely does raise the hackles. We'll just catch our horses and collect our cattle and be gone," he finished.

Behind him Randall stood to his full height and dusted himself off and glared in the direction Nate had taken, his eyes as hard as chips of flint.

Chapter Eighteen

Nate made it back to the herd at a fast gallop. He rode up to the chuckwagon and began an easy conversation with Charlie, who was still setting up for the evening.

"Where at's Mr. Randall? Heard you may've had some trouble," Charlie enquired.

"It's all sorted now. He wants me to head out and scout for sign. I may be gone a couple of days, so I'll take my bedroll," Nate explained cautiously.

Charlie looked puzzled but brought the roll from the wagon bed and watched as Nate strapped it to his saddle. He knew he couldn't waste any time, as Ted would soon be across to ask questions. With his bedroll secured, Nate rode to the remuda and got one of the wranglers to bring out Buck. He quickly transferred his saddle to the fresh horse and was about to be off when Steve appeared. It was getting tight, he knew.

"Nate, everythin' okay?" he called in a friendly manner.

"Sure, Steve, just heading out to do some scouting, need both my horses."

"Okay. Where's the others? I heard that there may have been a ruckus?"

"No, it's all taken care of and I'm scouting for Old Man Randall." Then he made a decision because he hated deceiving people. Mounting, he said: "Steve, I may be gone for a while. Keep at your reading and writing, you're doing well. Oh, and say hi to Billy Jo and Frank for me and tell them not to believe all they hear, will you do that for me?"

"Sure thing. You leavin' us?" Steve asked, puzzled.

"Yes, but keep it quiet for as long as you can, okay? Now I must be gone." With that he reached down and shook Steve's calloused hand, then gently touched his lower leg to Buck, who shot off, glad to be free of the remuda.

Nate rode north, but his instinct told him that he had to ensure that the farmer and his family were safe and had not been harassed further by Old Man Randall and his hands. So once out of sight of the herd, he swung west, making his way through brush and rocks on an old game trail, back to the farmer's homestead, hitting the earlier trail some five miles deeper into the valley.

Seeing the homestead, he circled further around to approach from the east, keeping out of sight until he was certain that the three DR Connected men were long gone. He saw more horses hitched outside but he didn't recognize any of them.

"Hello the house!" he called, sitting his horse, the thong off his Colt just in case, always recalling Sam's words.

The door opened and the blonde woman appeared again with a shotgun in her arms and two strangers at her back.

"What do you want? Oh, it's you." She changed as she recognized Nate.

Nate touched his Stetson in greeting. "Yes, ma'am, I just came back to see if everything was fine and that you were not hurt. How is your husband?" he asked gently.

"He is fine, thanks to you, just a sore neck and a li'l shook up. Sorry, where are my manners, please sit down and come in eat with us. We got company, so join us if you'd care to," she offered, lowering the shotgun.

"Much obliged, ma'am. I'll just see to my horses." With that he loosened the girth, let them drink and tied them up to a hitching rail away from the other horses.

"I'm Martha Jenkins. This here's my daughter Mary Lou and these gents are our neighbors Bob McBain and Abe Staple."

The daughter was the girl he'd seen on the porch earlier, and she was older and prettier than he had remembered. She was a girl ripening into full womanhood, with a mass of dark curls and pretty blue eyes. The other two were of a type, small-time ranchers with a tough frontier demeanor and sharp, wary eyes for any strangers that might bring trouble. They shook hands and moved into the main living area.

The house had a simple layout: a large main room for eating and living in with a kitchen area set around and a fireplace with an iron range upon which bubbled a stew that smelled mighty good to Nate. Two doors led off to the rear and a staircase had been partially built at the back, no doubt leading to an attic room to be constructed into the extended pitched roof. Everything was solidly made and designed, showing care and attention, yet it was homely and comfortable. Nate approved, seeing how it reflected the sort of people that they seemed to be—solid frontier folk forging a new life.

The man whose life he had saved earlier came forward. He had a raw red mark at his neck which he was bathing with a loose bandana that was wet with cold water.

"Mister, I want to thank you, I surely do, you saved my neck and no mistake. That was some fine shootin' for which I'm much obliged and to go agin' your boss like that took some courage. I'm Jim Jenkins, and I hope that you'll join us for supper and a bed if'n you're minded."

Nate shook his hand and introduced himself. No one, he was pleased to see, had any knowledge of him or the various shootings that he had been involved in, and he hoped that it would stay that way. Word had a habit in the west of flying along the prairie telegraph faster than a man could travel.

He was welcomed and as supper progressed they asked him about the herd, and what his plans were.

"Well, I don't know. I was hoping to see this drive out but clearly that was not meant to be. I need to go and see Old Man Randall and get my money as he has a hundred head of my cattle tied up with his, but apart from that I'm not really sure."

"You aren't tied anywhere, then?" Mary Lou asked. Nate had been aware that she had been hanging on his every word and giving him cows' eyes throughout the meal. Jim and Martha exchanged careful smiles, but said nothing, allowing their daughter her time.

"No, Miss Mary Lou, I'm not. I'm just drifting and trying to see some country and forget the war, I suppose. Maybe settle somewhere and do some ranching myself one day, who knows."

Then Jim cut across. "How'd you like to work for us?"

Nate frowned. "Can your spread run to a hired hand? I wouldn't have thought there'd be that much work for me."

"Not normally, no, but we—that is all the local spreads —we been doing a gather similar to that feller from the DR Connected, tho' much smaller. But we got ourselves some five hundred head together, maybe more and we want to run 'em up to market. Need a man who knows trailin' and can trail boss the herd."

McBain went red in the face. "Now see here, Jim, we discussed this and I thought we'd agreed that I would boss it and get the cattle to market. You don't know this feller, why he could still be workin' for them to take our herd. You don't know him from Adam," he finished angrily.

Before Nate could respond, Jim cut in. "Bob, you're a guest at my table, same as this young man, so you'll mind what you say afore you go bad mouthing someone. Yes, we talked about it but nothing was decided. And you don't know no more about drivin' cattle than me, or any of the other local boys. This man has been on the trail with more cows than we could shake a damn stick at."

Red faced, McBain turned to Nate. "Sorry, mister, no offence, but I don't know you and I don't know if'n you can do the job. It's not just my cattle and it ain't just Jim's either. It's all our cattle and we'd be stakin' our future on someone we don't know."

"He wouldn't be ridin' alone, Bob. We'd be there along-side him. So what do you say, Nate? Are you interested?" he said, turning back to Nate again.

Nate looked down at the table then up again, thinking quickly. It was an interesting opportunity, and it would get him north and paid for. He had learned a lot on the DR Connected drive over the last few weeks and reckoned he could manage a herd about a sixth of the size easily enough. There was an expectant silence around the table as he made up his mind. His contrary nature was as much made up by McBain's outburst as anything, but was that a good enough reason to take the offer?

"Well, I may be interested. But if I do boss it, then that is what I'll be—the Trail Boss, with no one telling me what to do or arguing. As many of you can come with me as you'd like, but it's my way or no way." At this he looked straight at McBain, who was not happy.

"Right then, I'll get the local people together and we'll put it to a vote. Either way you can stay the night with us and we'll see in the morning. We'll get together at Cork Crossing and have a meeting in the church and then we'll know. How's that sound?"

"Fine by me, I have no other plans. Whatever happens, I thank you for your hospitality."

"There's some fresh baked apple pie now for dessert, so you just set and I'll fetch it," Mary Lou offered. Nate gave her his best smile as she blushed and scurried to the stove.

The next morning Nate set off with Jim to the local town of Cork Crossing and was escorted to the church, a whitewashed building set in the center of a small picket fence on the outskirts of the town. Here all the local men had gathered to meet and make their decision. It didn't take long. He was ushered out after an introduction and few questions by various members of the group.

He sauntered down the street to find the café that he had spotted on the way in, where he ordered a pot of tea, which he still preferred over coffee whenever he could get it. He sat there contemplating how his life was about to change direction again. Then the bell above the door tinkled, admitting Jim who was grinning.

"Looks like you're in," he stated. "Time to go back and get better acquainted with all the folks."

Nate agreed the terms and began to draw up articles similar to those he had signed for the DR Connected drive. All fifteen of the local spread owners signed them, including a belligerent Bob McBain, who was still miffed at not having been voted trail boss himself. Nate was now officially in that position. He stood outside on the steps afterwards, thinking how his life had changed with the flip of a coin and moved on. Here he was, months after returning from the war, bossing his own drive with the knowledge he'd learned along the way. Then he got to thinking about Sam and was saddened by the news of his death. He had liked the Texan and owed him much. He sighed, replaced his hat and waited for Jim so they could ride home and make last minute preparations for the drive.

Chapter Nineteen

The next two days were frantic with activity as Nate tried to make sure that he brought together every bit of knowledge he'd gained on the drive north with the DR Connected. There were a number of huge differences and problems to overcome, which he explained to Jim Jenkins.

"The plan's pretty strong in a lot of ways but there are certain things that we need to consider hard." He raised his first finger. "We have enough men, but they are not experienced. Hopefully they'll pick it up quickly enough, but it's the horses that worry me more. We don't have enough, and what we do have aren't cutting horses. We'll be working them to a frazzle even though it's less than three hundred miles. Even if we make twelve miles a day, that's still more than three weeks pushing those dogies north over some rough and hostile country."

"Less than three hundred miles? Abilene's surely more'n that," Jim pointed out.

"It is, but we're not going to Abilene. We're going to

Dodge City. I was talking to one of the men here, Jas Box, used to scout for the army. He knows the route and says it would be better this time of year. I agree with him. We won't be eating dust and forcing the cattle to follow a trail of used up grass after the DR Connected. It's a clean route and it's much shorter. Harder at times, but it can be done. And Dodge is just as starved for beef as anywhere, if not more so. They'd welcome us and we'd likely get a better price than we would in Abilene after Randall's herd gets there and crowds out the market. Also, I know a cattle buyer, man by the name of Paul Tranter. I trust him and I'll cable him to see if he'll buy the stock. He was heading to Dodge last time I heard, and he'll tell me the lie of the land if nothing else."

"The horses are a problem for sure, but we'll see if we can't buy some on the way. There must be some cow ponies for sale along the trail," Jim replied.

"I hope so, or we'll kill our horses trying to keep up. The remuda is just too small."

"Okay, what else?" Jim asked.

"We'll need a wrangler for the remuda. We also need two wagons, one as a chuck wagon, one as a bed wagon. More importantly, who's going to drive them, who's going to cook and be the cook's louse?

"The hands can't do it, they'll be dead beat and desperate for grub as soon as they come in, and if we hit bad weather—which we will sure as eggs are eggs—we're going to need someone who can stick it out and serve hot grub come what may. We might rope in one or two of the young lads as wranglers, but a cook's going to be harder to find. All the able-bodied men will be on the drive and only McBain and maybe one or two others have got an extra hired hand, and then only two. The rest will be kept minding their places back here."

Jim raised his hands in dismay and seemed ready to reply, but he was silenced by another voice from the kitchen range.

"I can do it, Papa, you know I can," Mary Lou said.

"You? Don't you be so foolish, girl!" Jim admonished her.

"Why not?" she stated vehemently, showing to Nate's eyes great spirit. "I can cook, I'm young and strong and can handle a team of mules as well as anyone. Mama's showed me all her recipes and I can cook real well. I can make biscuits and stew as good as the best of them. I can tend to doctoring if anyone gets sick, too. I've mended busted bones and broken fevers since I was knee high."

Jim sat there open mouthed, but was suddenly outvoted.

"She's right, Jim," his wife chimed in. "She can do it and there'd be less to do here. You're takin' all the stock bar the milk cows and the young 'uns. Billy can help me with 'em and see to the chores."

"Well damn it, Martha, why not take Billy as well? I mean he's ten, for God's sake, we should have ourselves some toddlers for the trail, too," he ranted in exasperation. "And where in tarnation do we get a cook's louse, huh? Who's going to share a wagon with our daughter? Have you thought of that, all together cooped up day and night!" he shouted. "I'll not have it."

Nate looked on, swearing he would never get married or get on the wrong side of the womenfolk.

"What about Rusty? She'd come and keep me company at night," Mary Lou said calmly.

"Rusty?" Nate asked.

"Archie McAllister's daughter," Jim replied. "Archie runs one of the neighboring farms. You probably met him at the meeting."

Nate vaguely recalled a friendly red-haired man with a firm handshake.

"Me an' her are best friends and she's a real tomboy," Mary Lou enthused. "She'll do any man's work and more, and she can ride anything with hair."

Jim threw up his hands in despair, shaking his head in disbelief. "I'll not have it, d'ya hear me? I'll not have it." He thrust his hat on and stomped out of the house into the fading light.

Mary Lou looked on, crestfallen.

"You leave your father to me, dear." Martha sighed, patting Mary Lou's hand. "What do you say, Nate? Do you have any objections?"

"Ma'am, I'm plumb out of other options. If the girls can do it—and I mean really do it, not just have a lark—if they're prepared to be shouted at if they make mistakes, with no sides taken or favors given, then yes, I agree." Nate turned to Mary Lou. "But I warn you, missy, one whimper, one sign of weakness or getting all female on me and I will be down on you with a heavy hand just like you were a man. We clear?" he said.

"Yes, Mr. Carlton, we sure are. Now let me ride over and talk to Rusty. Please, Ma?"

"It's late..." Martha began to protest.

"Ma'am, time's short and we need this settled. I'll ride with Mary Lou and talk to Rusty's father, and we'll be back in no time. Trust me, I'll look after her and her friend, but I need to settle this."

Nate and Mary Lou saddled their horses and set off into the gathering gloom towards the McAllister homestead. Nate was not sure what he was getting himself involved in, but he was determined that this was a serious business, and he would flatly refuse to consider the girls as hands of any sort at the first sign of any tantrums or skittishness. A cattle drive was no place for a woman, it was hard and sometimes deadly work, and many men never finished a drive, falling to accidents and sickness along the trail. But he was desperate and had no alternative but to humor Mary Lou. They made short work of the journey, each with their own thoughts and little said, and on the way Nate noted that Mary Lou was a natural rider who sat her saddle well and managed her horse as confidently as any trail hand.

They arrived at the McAllister homestead just as night was falling and shouted across to the house so as not to alarm anyone. The door was opened to reveal the redheaded man Nate remembered from town, carrying an oil lamp.

"Is that you, Mary Lou? Somethin' wrong to bring you callin' at such a time?" he asked, concerned.

"It's me and Mr. Nate Carlton. We've come to see you and Rusty."

"Well come on in, then. Coffee's on the stove and we've just eaten, but there's some leftover pie if'n you've a mind." He welcomed them, raising the lamp high as they dismounted and tied their horses to the rail.

The inside of the house looked much like the Jenkins' home; warm, snug and comfortable with the fresh smell of blueberry pie and coffee. Nate was introduced to McAllister's wife, a fair-haired woman, and three girls, all redheads. The twins would be about twelve years old, Nate estimated, and the older girl, Rusty, was the same age as Mary Lou. She was shorter and a little plump but had a look of strength to her shoulders and toned arms that showed she was clearly no stranger to hard work. Her hair was wild and wiry, she had clear blue eyes and a sprinkling of freckles across the bridge of her upturned nose.

"Hey, Rusty gal," Mary Lou greeted her with a hug. "We all got some talking to do and I'll think you'll like it."

Rusty arched an eyebrow and smiled at her friend and Nate got the distinct impression that she already knew how the conversation was going to go. He wasn't sure that McAllister was going to like it quite so much, but the poor man must be henpecked to Hell and back with four women in the house. He was probably hoping for a boy—but the twins were already twelve, so he'd maybe given up on the whole idea.

Coffee and pie served, they sat at the table and Nate explained what had occurred with Mary Lou and the shortage of men. Mary Lou stayed silent until the end, then jumped in persuasively, saying what a good idea it was and how they would be an asset.

As Nate guessed, McAllister looked at his wife for guidance before he spoke up. "Ain't no denying that we're short of menfolk to get the drive done and at least you would keep each other company safely in the wagons. What does your pappy say, Mary Lou?"

"Oh, he's all for it," she replied. "Long as you agree to let Rusty come along, too."

Nate nearly choked on his coffee and spluttered a little, looking sideways at Mary Lou, whose face was as schooled as that of a riverboat gambler.

"Well then, that settles it," Mrs. McAllister said. "You go along, Rusty girl, and do us proud. Your father'll be there as well to make sure you don't come to no harm, and me and the girls can handle the farm while you're gone."

"Marge, are you sure?" McAllister asked.

"I'm plumb certain. Girl's stronger than most boys her age and she's got a good head on her shoulders. She can ride and ribbon a team with the best of 'em," Marge said proudly. Turning to Nate, she said: "She'll do you proud, and no complaints mind, girl, you listen to the trail boss and all will be well."

"Yes, Mama, I surely will," Rusty exclaimed, her eyes alight with excitement, apparently not at all surprised by the turn of events, confirming Nate's suspicions.

The talk then flowed fast with all agreeing to meet up in two days' time, the day before the herd was due to start out.

The next two days were a busy time for everyone. Men came in from all over, herding small numbers of cattle before them. Each addition was counted, and Nate noted the numbers and brands in the tally book, double checking them with Jim. The McAllisters appeared a day early, driving their meagre herd. The cattle were in good shape and well fed, with no muleys, Nate was pleased to see. Rusty handled the ribbons of the wagon she drove with an easy skill, and whatever else Nate's misgivings might be, she could certainly handle the team of mules that pulled it. The axles were freshly greased, the cover new and all seemed set.

In all they had eighteen men plus two youngsters to look after the remuda. Nate had the younger hands practice the difficult task of handling the cable corral for the drive that would serve to keep the horses together at night. They had managed to beg, steal and borrow a few more horses, some less skilled than others. Nate prayed that it would be enough.

McBain, he noted, was still belligerent, and Nate decided to keep a wary eye upon him, keen to nip any trouble in the bud before it really started. There was little more he could do, and he made a special effort to be amenable and friendly until—and indeed if—McBain started any trouble. He could not condemn the man simply for being miserable.

Then the day arrived. The cattle had been held in a natural draw, enclosed on three sides by a manmade thorn and cactus hedge with a small stream running through it. The grass had all gone, and they were restless, keen to move out in search of more grass. The timing was perfect, Nate decided.

The thorn hedge was pushed back, and the first drag riders went to the back and started to haze the cattle as the point, swing and flank riders waited to receive the herd. They were all still a little unsure as to how it would all work, but they were ready to try their best.

Mary Lou hugged her mother and her kid brother goodbye as Nate stayed to the side, with Jas Box having gone ahead as the ex-army scout knew the land really well. Nate felt shivers of anticipation run down his spine. It was happening again, the thrill of a drive, smaller this time, but the thrill of seeing all these cattle head north, now under his orders, was the same. Looking at Mary Lou and Rusty as they urged the wagons forward, he was again aware of the massive responsibility that had been placed upon his young shoulders.

Chapter Twenty

For two days Nate followed the rules he'd learned from the DR Connected drive. Pushing the cattle hard to get them off home ground, he finally eased up on the third day. The farmers were not as used to riding all hours in the saddle as regular cowhands, and most were tired and sore, collapsing into their bedrolls at the end of a hard day.

"Are we goin' to keep pushin' 'em like this all the drive?" McBain asked aggressively as darkness fell around the campfire.

"Only tomorrow, then we'll ease up quite a bit," Nate replied. "They'll settle, they'll be tired, and once they're off the home range they'll be much more manageable. You'll see, it'll be fine."

"Yeah? Well, I don't think you know what you're doin', sonny." McBain sneered.

Here it comes, Nate thought, and brought steel into his voice: "Well, mister, I really don't give a good goddamn what you think. You are on this drive as a hired hand. You've got a vested interest, certainly, but that's where it ends. Once we get to Dodge you can do and think what you like, but out here I'm the trail boss and you signed up to the rules. Now take it or leave it." Nate stood and threw the dregs out of his coffee cup into the fire with a sharp hiss, waiting for a response. It was a direct challenge, and he knew he had to meet it head on. He had seen non-coms in the war have the same battles with uppity enlisted men.

"Says you, standing there in your fancy rig. A gun slick, so I heard. Killed a man down in Texas and a few others, I'm bound. How do you stack up without your Colt, huh?"

Nate knew it would happen sometime. Someone would test him. McBain was big and beefy and stood raising his fists. A tense air of expectancy rose around the camp. None had seen this challenge coming so soon, but as western men they all knew that a title was not enough, and often it needed backing up.

But Jim stood up. "Why don't you back off, McBain, you've been grumbling since this all started."

"Hah! Getting Jim to fight your battles for you now, Carlton?" He sneered.

"No. It's my fight, McBain, and you called it. So you either apologize or we'll set to. Your choice," Nate said calmly.

"What about your gun?" McBain teased.

"I won't need that for a loudmouthed milksop like you." Nate laughed at him. He wanted McBain angry and careless, and he got both.

"Why you...!" McBain shouted and rushed in with his head lowered to smash Nate in the stomach, going to smother him and brutalize him with work-hardened fists of iron.

Nate was pleased and judged the moment well. He saw the man was no brawler, he was all brawn and anger with no science to it. He waited two paces and when his opponent was in range he kicked up fast, right between McBain's legs. The man looked as though he had run into a steam train. He staggered one more step and as he did so, Nate locked his hands together and smashed them down on McBain's exposed neck. McBain dropped limp to the floor as though he had been poleaxed, his rasping breath the only clue that he was still alive.

"You two." Nate pointed to McBain's hands. "Get him up, fetch a bucket of water and cool him off. Anyone else object to me running the drive the way I am?" He looked around.

"You never gave him a chance, Nate, that was brutal," Jim said, astounded at what he had just seen.

"This isn't Queensbury Rules. If we have a ruckus here and spook the cattle we all lose out because one loudmouth wants to cause trouble. I dealt with him quickly and quietly, and all he'll do is be galled by his saddle for a day or so and have himself a headache. No real harm done. Now we have a drive to run to get the cattle to market. That's what you are paying me for, not to make friends with everyone.

"Mary Lou," he said curtly and suddenly, turning away as though the conversation was finished. "Make sure your wagon is tongued and faces the North Star, like I told you yesterday." He realized, as he had during the war, that being in command is a lonely position with few if any friends. She gave him a scornful look that was at odds with the way she'd looked at him before the trail had started, as though abashed by his sharpness. He understood how responsibility changed a man, and knew it was happening again. Was he getting harder with all that had happened to him, he wondered? He would be no more than two or three years older than her, yet he felt like an old man in comparison.

She answered with spunk: "Yes, sir, mister Trail Boss." She stormed off to follow his orders before he could reply. In a way he was pleased. He thought that she'd been developing a crush on him and if he could stop that and get this done efficiently they'd both be the better for it. This was a harsh land and it needed harsh men and methods to govern it and see everything through.

Mary Lou strode off to the chuck wagon, and with Rusty's help they aligned the shafts with the North Star so that they would know in the morning which way to go.

"That was brutal. He didn't give Bob McBain a chance, he just cut him down so casually with two blows as though he had planned what he was going to do before poor Bob even made a move. I thought he was nice and easy going, too," Mary Lou commented.

"So did I," Rusty replied. "But he couldn't risk spooking the herd and McBain was asking for it. He's a mean man himself, I saw him bust up two men in a brawl once at a dance, do you remember? Reckons he's a tough hombre. But what did he mean about Nate killing a man down in Texas? You heard anything?"

"No, but I wonder what kind of man he really is. He's an Englishman, that much I do know, you can hear it in his voice. I saw him shoot the rope around Pa's neck and face down his boss and two other gunnies, all calm as though it were a walk in the woods."

"He's no stranger to trouble, that's for sure, and he don't let no one get too close. I wonder what his story is?" Rusty said.

The girls carried on speculating about Nate and talking about what had happened, then when all were fed and the dishes washed off, they tumbled into the wagon to sleep.

That night as he bedded down, Nate pulled his Colt into the suggan, ready just in case. It was going to be a long drive, he decided.

The next day they all woke with the dawn. The girls were up with a fire blazing and hot coffee and breakfast on the go.

"Do you see much of interest ahead yesterday, Jas?" Nate asked, squinting over the steam of a scalding cup of coffee.

"Waal now, we head sorta north northwest, through a break in the hills that-a way." He gestured with his hand. Like most western plainsmen, he carried a map in his head, rarely forgetting a feature or a useful marker. In a land with few formal maps, it was a necessary skill that western men developed over time. "Then there are two small rivers to cross but we won't hit the second for two more days if we slow down like your plannin' to after you explained it so nicely to mister McBain last night." He chuckled.

"He had it coming. He's been pushing and jockeying for position since I got into the mix of things. Better to get it sorted now and with no gunplay. Nothing more than a bruised ego."

"Ain't that the truth. He reckons he's the old bull of the

woods around here. Big fish, small pond. He larned, though, he surely did." Jas nodded.

"Right, I'll take a scout today. You take point and then head out and watch the flanks, will you. Just in case there's any trouble brewing. I heard talk of herd cutters with the DR Connected. They're a tough bunch by all accounts, and they may well see us as a soft target."

Jas tipped his hat. "Will do, boss. See you later." He swilled the remains of his coffee out of the tin mug, passed it to Mary Lou who was standing nearby, mounted up and rode off at a gentle lope to the head of the herd.

"You two all set?" he asked the girls, in a gentler manner than the previous evening.

"Sure, we're ready and waiting," Rusty answered.

Good. You see that butte over there about ten miles way? We'll head for that. You'll pass through and we'll camp the other side tonight. Jas says there's a river nearby, so it'll be good for water and fuel. I'll be scouting around so I might bump into you. Any problem, of any kind, you fire three fast shots with your rifle, anything at all untoward, got it?"

"Sure," Mary Lou answered. "You expectin' trouble?" she asked, looking slightly worried.

"Jas and I have seen tracks, both shod and unshod. Could be nothing, but best be careful and keep that rifle handy. If you see anything in the way of tracks, being as you're ahead of the herd, remember and let me know tonight, all right?"

They both nodded. He gave them a tight smile, mounted up and rode off.

The day rolled on, and as they reached the butte they

took a head count. It tallied with the counts given by each homesteader, plus two that they had already picked up along the way. These were branded in Nate's name as had been agreed at the meeting.

They pushed on through the gap to the river, which they crossed in the way Nate had learned, spreading the herd to avoid crowding. On the other side they found the camp the two girls had set up. Nate rode up from the west, where he had been scouting.

"You two alright?"

"No, these are the ghosts from our bodies that the trail boss left after working us too hard!" Rusty retorted.

"Well, you surely smell ripe enough. How long have you been dead, a week?" Nate responded in kind, pleased to be back on an even keel with the girls.

"Didn't we say something about puttin' grit in the trail boss's supper, Mary Lou?"

"We surely did, less'n he'd like to go hungry." Mary Lou grinned innocently.

Nate held up his hands for peace, giving in and taking a plate of hot food. "Okay, now did you see any tracks at all?"

"We did. A horse—shod, mind—crossed the trail ahead of the herd passing west to northeast just through the butte. Fresh tracks by the look of it," Rusty offered.

"Just one?"

"Yep, why?"

"Could be a scout for herd cutters. They do that, so I've heard, start tracking the herds early so they can be ready. Well now, I'll be extra vigilant. Thank you, good work."

For two weeks they continued to push the herd, and each

day Nate and Jas got the feeling they were being watched. Twice more the tracks of a lone horse were spotted, but there was no sighting of the rider or his animal. Whoever the man was, he was keeping himself below the skyline and was careful to stay far enough away never to be caught. The sun got hotter and the cattle became more tired as the need for water became a pressing matter. They were the first herd up this trail, so the grass was good, but everyone was tired and so were the horses.

"I don't like it, Jas," Nate said. "I think we're in for trouble when we get a few miles short of Dodge City, probably just before the Ford County line."

Chapter Twenty-One

The unshod horses had been circling now for a while, and the first sign of Indians came two days later. A group of Cherokee appeared over a ridge and made their way down the gentle slope to the side of the herd.

"Where there's some there'll be more," Jas opined.

"Take Jim, the Sutler boy, and McBain's man Rory. He was a buffalo hunter has a Sharps and he's a good shot with a rifle. If I take my hat off and wave left to right, you take out the leader. But—and take care here—if I point to the ground you shoot between them, just to frighten them and let them know we mean business. Watch for my signal. Now, get to the high ground, go!" Nate told him.

Jas needed no second bidding and wheeled away to pick the men Nate had named. He watched carefully as they moved back, and then in a careless action of looking back at the herd he noticed that they'd slipped behind a mesa and disappeared from sight. He hoped that they would be in place in time.

"Jake," he said to one of the young hands, "get up and tell the girls to be ready. First sign of trouble tell them to stop the wagons and get out of sight. We'll be up for them. Wait," he added as the young hand made to ride off, "tell them to put their hair up and pull their hats low, and wear vests or coats to disguise themselves. If these Indians know we have women along things'll be harder." Luckily they were wearing pants for the drive, not skirts. Hopefully it would be enough, and he prayed that they did not fall into Indian hands.

"Yes, sir!" Jake shouted in response. "I'll look to 'em, Nate, don't you worry none."

As usual, the chuck and bedroll wagons were ahead of the herd but had only just taken this position as the day neared its end so that they could set up camp for the night. Jake, who was but sixteen himself, shot off at a gallop to close the distance with the wagons. He was a steady hand, Nate knew, mature beyond his years, and Nate had been teaching him to shoot on the quiet. He hoped that he would stand firm. Then he motioned with his hand for the herd to stop, and the point closed them down and kept them boxed in. Everyone was nervous and expectant, tensions were high.

"Have your weapons ready," Nate shouted to them. "Don't draw unless I say, but keep the rifles across your saddles in sight and ready. I want no trouble unless they start it. The herd will spook given half a chance and I'd rather lose a few head on a trade than half to a stampede."

All in hearing nodded and passed the word back.

The raiding party, for that was what it seemed to be, galloped up, sliding their ponies to a halt in a dramatic fashion in a haze of dust. Nate counted fifteen or so warriors of mixed age, with some young bucks out to prove themselves. It was these Nate watched closely. They were mostly armed with the bows and spears for which the Cherokee were famous. A few had rifles lifted from the white man, probably dead soldiers after the war, Nate supposed, and they had adorned them with the usual tacks studded into the stocks. The leading brave was not a full war bonnet chief but controlled the rest and had what looked like an Army Colt holstered in a flapped cavalry twist holster at his side. He was proud and had the paint of a senior brave. Nate gave one last look at the wagons to make sure the girls were safe then turned his full attention upon him.

He made the sign for peace and friendship learned from scouts in the war and sat ready for the response. He knew some sign language and saw the chief brave respond in kind. Nate made the sign for trade and the chief responded in guttural Cherokee.

"You speak Cherokee?"

"A little, and a little sign. I am Nate Carlton."

"I am Hawk Circling." He made a motion high into the air.

"What do you need?" Nate responded, reinforcing his rusty Cherokee with sign language.

"You have many beef and two wagons—full of food and guns, maybe?"

Nate schooled his features. It was the old game; Indians loved to trade and negotiate. Any sign of weakness would result in a battle, one he did not want, for either way they would lose stock.

The talk continued, with Jim trying to interrupt: "Nate, we should just shoot 'em," he muttered.

"Button it, Jim!" Nate snapped from the side of his mouth, looking at the chief man all the time.

He swore he saw a flicker of an expression too fleeting to gauge pass across the man's eyes. Nate continued as though nothing had been said, but the chief surprised Nate by switching to English. He had been playing a game, seeking an advantage to see what he could learn. "Where you learn Cherokee?" he demanded.

Nate controlled his emotions, thankful that he had silenced Jim. He told him slowly and in great detail, the way the Indians liked to hear things. The more of a story, the better they liked it. At length he finished, and silence reigned. He was still unsure which way this was going to go.

He saw the chief look around, summing up how many men he had and what his chances were of stealing the wagons and some cows. "You have few men. I think we take cows and wagons as payment for riding through our land."

"Chief." He flattered him but also put a harsh tone to his voice. "If you try to do that you will not see the day to eat the beef." With this he raised his hat and pointed to the ground in front of them, hoping that Rory was ready and saw his sign.

The chief frowned, about to get angry, then a loud report from a heavy caliber rifle echoed across the plain. It was followed by a *whup* as the .50 caliber Sharps bullet buried itself into the ground between them. The Indian ponies shied a little, as did the two of the hands that we close by.

"The next one will hit you. You may get me, but we all have repeating rifles and the wagons ahead have three men all with Henrys ready, willing, and able to kill any who try to take them. You may have more men hidden, but we do too, up in the hills," he bluffed.

The chief smiled. "You are clever and wise white man, Nate Carlton. A Cherokee taught you well."

"So why don't we settle down? We will trade with you, share some food, and you can stay the night. In the morning we'll see you right with some beef and we'll all be on our way."

The brave motioned to his men, who turned to fall in with the point riders as the herd began to move off again.

Jim sidled up to Nate. "You sure you know what you're doin'?" Jim asked quietly.

"I certainly hope so. The Cherokee are our guests, and it's better to have them in here with us where we can keep an eye on them, and they'll feel an obligation to be honorable and neighborly. Now I want you to ride ahead in a minute." Nate looked up at the gathering dark clouds that were knitting together as a cold front pushed across the plains, bringing with it a strange light that was almost shaded in its tinge, with a faint yellow hue. "There's rain coming, I can taste it. I am going to ask you loudly to ride ahead, but first listen. When you get there, make sure the girls have slickers on and ready. Have them put dirt on their faces and pull their hats down low. They're to have as little contact with the Indians as possible. Get Jake to help with the food and serve it out, not them." He then made to turn away and in a louder voice as though as an afterthought said: "Jim, you head on up to the wagons and tell the men to have more grub ready. We have company tonight, so make sure they get it good and hot."

Jim, to his credit, nodded as though this was the first he heard of it and cantered off in the direction of the wagons ahead. As he did so the first spots of rain started to fall, and all around pulled out their slickers or hide ponchos for the Indians.

It had gone better than Nate had hoped, and the weather helped. Everyone was subdued but wary. The night herd was doubled, and the girls were kept out of sight as much as possible away from the direct firelight and always in the shadows. Jake would be on fire duty and Nate would take a spell himself, as he didn't trust the girls to be exposed and wanted it kept going all night despite the steadily falling rain. The men pulled up the tarps around their suggans in an effort to stay as dry as possible. The cattle were calm; there was no thunder, just a steady spring rain.

"Rory, I want you and another under the bedroll wagon, keep your gun handy and pretend you're asleep."

"Sure, boss. You'll get no argument from me there. Best place to be on a night like this, apart from actually in the wagon," Rory joked and went off to get another man to help stand watch with him.

"Jas, I want you out there tonight, and keep wary. It's a hard job but you'll spot the trouble ahead of the others if it comes."

"Sure, Nate, anything you say."

"Rusty? You and Lou there keep the wagon and food dry, spell each other, alright?" Nate made a big thing about this, making sure all heard and using just Mary Lou's second name to keep up the pretense. Then, once all was secure he rolled up under the cook wagon next to Jake, facing away from the fire at the harness end of the wagon. Jake faced the other way so both men could guard the girls within.

All was silent within the camp, everyone seemingly asleep, drifting off to the sound of the rain hissing as it hit the coals of the fire that still burned steadily. In the early morning the rain stopped as quickly as it had started. It was still dark and the glow of dawn was yet to appear on the horizon.

Nate was asleep but something woke him, bringing him to consciousness with an unknowing part of his brain that warned him that something was amiss. He kept still but carefully opened one eye, squinting about the camp. Then he saw it—a shadow rose and slipped towards the fire on soft moccasined feet. It was one of the young bucks, heading seemingly out of the camp circle through the loose ring of sleeping men. Another figure stirred and made to rise, joining his fellow brave, who had now circled and was making for the outside of the wagon.

He'll cut the canvas. Maybe he knows there's women in there and I wasn't clever enough, Nate thought. He had to act now, he knew, without causing a firefight, for all would be lost. He gambled, stretching and yawning as though just waking from sleep and said in voice that carried, "Jake, it's your turn to stoke the fire."

To be fair to the youngster, Jake was awake quickly enough and caught on fast, rising slowly and giving the brave time to re-think his actions. He stood, stamping his feet into his boots with a show of getting up.

Then Nate also rose. "Damned if I don't have to go now. Must be all that coffee," he muttered. "Best take my pistol, might meet a bear or snake." He shoved it into his waist belt, knowing he was being watched by the second Indian who had just risen, then he made his way forward to the fire and casually placed a couple of small logs onto the glowing coals. He looked up and smiled at Rory, who went to join him. With the noise of movement, others stirred, seeing the drama play out before them. They all knew what was going on, and no surprise would now be had, or virtue of the girls taken, if indeed that had been the young Indians' intention. But no man trusted opportunity, and an Indian would sometimes take it.

As Nate left the circle, he squinted into the dark and saw the first Indian coming back, acting innocently enough.

"How," Nate said, making to unbutton his pants with his left hand, "you too, huh?" he added, smiling. Now he was certain, larceny or worse had been planned.

The brave just nodded, his face inscrutable, but both men knew how close it had been. Nate finished and made his way back cautiously, then stuck his head inside the wagon.

"Lou, you and the louse best get up early. We've hungry men to feed and it'll be a long day what with rain and every-thing." He spoke quietly, but loud enough for those who were awake to hear.

There were muffled grunts from inside and the sound of movement. Now everybody knew that the camp was alert. Another disaster averted, Nate thought.

Chapter Twenty-Two

The dawn arrived shortly afterwards with the promise of a sunny day to follow the rain. The trade was concluded: some old rifles, ten head of beef and a few pouches of tobacco. It was, Nate reflected, a small price to pay for not losing half a herd or even their lives on the trail.

The Indians made to leave at just after dawn. The assembled braves looked on, pleased with their cattle, but none were fooled. The head of the raiding party, Hawk Circling, came before Nate, made the sign for friend and smiled faintly. Everyone knew what had occurred and each kept his own secrets and council.

"I thank you for your food and trade, white man. Maybe we shall see each other again."

"I hope so, Chief, in peace as always, for you are always welcome at my camp."

"You will be known to our people as a man of honor." With that, Hawk Circling bowed and led his party away without a backward glance. All in the camp let out a collective sigh of relief.

"Man, you sure do play a fair hand of poker. Remind me not to play with you!" Jim stated.

"Amen to that," Rory said. "You surely got their measure. I could see my scalp hanging at one of their lodge-poles for a time back there."

Nate, embarrassed at the compliments, deflected them in his usual manner. "Gentlemen, while it's lovely to start the morning with a genial chat and some friendly bonhomie, I do believe that we have a herd to get to market. Now move 'em out!" His last words were a shouted command.

"And there he be, the trail boss returns," moaned Mary Lou, sighing and shaking her head.

The others laughed at this and made to break camp in a hurry, heeding Nate's commands.

Mary Lou stood at the side of the chuck wagon watching Nate's silhouette recede into the morning light, and might have stayed there longer had Rusty not nudged her in the ribs.

The cattle were soon roused and another day of pushing them forward began. The days passed and just over three weeks from when they had first started the drive they rode over the Ford County Line. Everyone was tired, but they were also euphoric, as Buffalo City was only about a day's drive away. All had made it pretty much unscathed. One boy, Saul, had been galled by an errant steer, breaking his leg, and he now rode the chuck wagon, his limb in a splint and set well by Mary Lou, who had done all she had promised, making a good team with Rusty.

Nate was still wary of getting too close to her. She allowed a special smile to flash across her pretty face when he came near, despite having been harsh with her at times for any shortcomings in her duties. Both girls had been as good as any regular cook and louse, never failing to have a hot meal ready in all conditions. Nate sidled up to the wagon as it rolled along parallel to the head of the herd. They were now easing ahead as the day came to a close, looking to the place where they would make camp and prepare supper. Nate wanted all to be well and complimented them on a job well done.

"Ladies, just in case I forget to say so later, you have both been remarkable. Every day you turned up trumps and kept us going. You can have a job in my trail team any day and we couldn't have done it without you. Now, when we get to Dodge I want you to do something for me. My treat."

Both girls looked on from the wagon seats, expectant but clearly puzzled, unsure if it was a joke or if Nate was serious.

"Okay, if this is a windy, we're ready for it. Come on, what's the joke?" Mary Lou said.

"There's no joke, and I'm really hurt that you think so..." Nate cast his eyes down.

"Mister Trail Boss, sir, bear in mind that you would like to eat dinner without no grit in it tonight, so would you please tell us all what you have in mind," Rusty called across, her tone full of sarcasm.

"Okay, I surrender. Well, ladies," he began gallantly, "as you have spent the whole drive wearing pants, and I am sure you're both really ladies underneath, I would like you to go into town, find an emporium and buy yourself a dress each on me."

There was stunned silence from both girls. "Are you serious? Really?" Mary Lou grinned at him.

"Oh yes, mister Carlton, sir, you can have some supper now," Rusty said. "But you'd better not welch on our deal."

"I won't. It's a promise. And I'll have a dance with each of you at the hoedown." With this he lifted his hat in mock salute and cantered off to chase a cow.

"Well blow me down. Is he being gallant?" Mary Lou asked.

"I think he is, Mary Lou, and we'll take him up on it. A store bought dress from Dodge City! Won't the girls back home be jealous?" Rusty whooped. With this elated feeling they whipped up the mules and headed at a quicker pace for the site that Jas had marked for tonight's camp. It was a flattish plain with woods sloping gently down from east and west, forming a natural wide corral in the open. Jas was waiting for them by a small stream that would provide water for cooking, and there was firewood from dead trees and windfalls of birch and oak.

The edges of the woodland were spruce and pine, and further along a few willows were nearly in full leaf, whispering and swaying in the gentle breeze as the air caught them, trailing their long yellow tendrils. It was a peaceful scene and a fitting end to the drive.

Everyone was in a joyful mood as the herd swung into the camp. Then Nate heard the sound of faster hooves as riders bore down from the western slope and cursed himself for a fool. He had relaxed too soon. No scouts were out, both he and Jas were with the herd talking over the plans for the next day. He looked around, Rory was on the flank and young Jake was near the wagon.

"McAllister," he shouted to Rusty's father. "Get to the wagon, get the girls safe. This is trouble or I miss my guess. Have them ready to fire, but stay under cover. Now go!"

"Rory, you and Jake with me. You too, Jim."

"I'm coming, too, Nate," Bob McBain said surprisingly. He had become more amendable since the fight, and had evidently seen the error of his ways. He signaled his other hand, Hank, to come along.

"Glad to have you, Bob. Right, pull your long guns, nothing acts as good a deterrent than a long gun close up. It'll certainly make a mess of a man and you're less likely to miss."

"I'll stick with my Colt, Nate," Jake offered. "You think it's trouble? Looks to be about fifteen or twenty of 'em."

"I do. I'll bet my wages these are the herd cutters everyone's been talking about, and they won't back down unless we give them a strong show of force, but we'll see how it all plays out first. They like to run off a herd close to town but outside the purview of the marshal. Then they'll bring 'em in from another direction or even another town all rebranded having killed or wounded most of the trail hands. They always hit when everyone feels safe, like now. I should have seen it coming. They're brutal and merciless, so shoot to kill and no conscience. Am I clear?" There were nods all round. "Good. But wait for my lead, spread out wide in a semi-circle, not bunched and leave me in front—and whatever happens leave the three front men to me," he ordered.

"Three?" Rory asked. "You reckon you're that good?"

"I'm not boasting, Rory, but I know what I need to do. Take the leaders, the rest will fold. No more talk now. Get in position, come up fast and slam to a halt, it'll unnerve them." He saw that McAllister was with the wagon and the girls were ready, their guns showing. They were now to the right and slightly forward of the party in front, with only about thirty yards between them. Nate did not like it as already three of the new arrivals were looking over at the wagon and the girls. The party set off, leaving as few behind as possible.

"Nate, be warned, that's Kurt Brannigan. I mind him from the war, when he rode with Quantrill," Rory said.

Nate nodded in response. Most had heard of Brannigan and knew him as one of the bloodiest and most infamous members of that cutthroat crew. If half the deeds associated with his name were true they were in for trouble, and Nate was worried for the girls. Normally a western man would leave women strictly alone, and men had been hung for molesting a woman, with a strict code in a land where women were few and far between and respected above all else. Even hardened outlaws would respect this. But not Quantrill and his crew, who had reputedly raped and pillaged their way across the states, with Brannigan leading by example.

They did as they were bidden and slid to a halt in front of the bunched group in front of them, throwing up dust and forcing the men opposite to control their mounts. Close to, they were a fearsome looking bunch, some of the roughest men Nate had ever seen. They reminded him in their demeanor of Craw Gillett and the men with him. They were evil, dressed in rough clothes and military cast offs of both blue and grey. They were unshaven, hard-eyed, and by their expressions they didn't seem to have an iota of mercy in their souls. All had belt guns, rode big powerful horses, and carried repeating rifles in their saddle scabbards. A couple of Sharps were evident. These were outlaws of the worst kind, with not an ounce of humanity in them. They would not be intimidated under any circumstances. Then Nate saw a shiny star upon the leader's vest that marked him as a deputy sheriff.

"Howdy," Nate began gently, appearing polite and a little cowed by the force before him.

"Sonny, I'm Sheriff Brannigan and you're in my baili-wick. I'm looking for the trail boss, where's he at?"

"Well, Sheriff," Nate began, sounding as mild and refined as he could, inflecting his English accent. "That would be me. My name is Nate Carlton, how may I be of service to you?"

"You?" Brannigan sneered, grinning round at his men. "You're the trail boss of this sorry looking outfit? Well, Mister Carlton. I've been appointed by the governor of Kansas to extract a head tax for all herds using this trail. That being said, you either pay eight dollars a head or we take cattle in lieu of payment. It's your choice, and I'm giving you the chance to make it as a duly appointed officer of the law."

"Well, sir. That ... um ... that seems to be an awful lot of money." Nate raised his hand to his hat and wiped his fore-head with his forearm as though uncomfortable. In doing so he dropped his right arm to cross over the saddle horn, resting there away from his right-hand Colt. He also allowed Buck to sidle slightly to the left. He sensed that the rest of his crew were puzzled, knowing how tough he could be. Only Rory was not fooled, he knew what was coming and inched his hand toward his own six gun. "Can we not trade in another form of payment, like the gentlemen we are?" Nate continued.

"Well now, seeing as how you're being all friendly 'n' that, I think we'll take what's in those wagons as well, as part payment." Brannigan let out an unpleasant hoot of laughter, as did his men, thinking that they had this soft talking dude beaten.

"That wasn't what I had in mind."

"What then?"

"Lead."

Nate's tone changed to ice, and the words hit home and reaction set in for Brannigan. But it was too late. The knowledge that he had been outplayed gave him insufficient time to react and change his mentality from predator to prey.

"Now," Brannigan shouted, dropping his hand to the Colt lying in the sash at his waist. Yet even as his hand grasped the ivory grips, the first of two .36 caliber bullets smashed into his chest, knocking him backward from his horse. Nate's Colt Police Special spat again, taking the second in command with a head shot, then he turned it on the third, whose pistol was just lining up, in a swirl of powder smoke. The gunman slid sideways from the saddle, his hands wide, gun dropping from lifeless fingers. Everything was chaos, men shooting all around him, acrid black powder smoke filling the air. The thought that he was back in the war again came unbidden into Nate's consciousness, the old memories returning, and with them the knowledge that he must move and keep moving.

He urged Buck forward, did a border shift to palm his Navy and came face to face with another gunman. He fired point blank and the man's face seemed to blow apart in a haze of blood. Nate heard shots over by the wagon and turned Buck with his legs, driving him forward through the pall of powder smoke. The wagon came into view, and he saw a gunman leveling a pistol at Mary Lou who was working the lever of a Henry rifle. Nate fired a snap shot and missed, but the hissing of the bullet alerted the outlaw to his presence as it passed, and he turned bringing his gun to bear on him. Both men fired at the same time. They both missed, but the gunman jerked forward, hit by the heavy rifle slug entering his back. Mary Lou had found her mark. A gunman lay prone on the floor dead and the third, who looked wounded, turned his horse and galloped away.

Nate jumped off his horse and ran to Mary Lou, who slumped in post battle reaction. "You alright, girl?" he asked, concerned, grabbing her by the shoulders.

"Yes, yes I..." Her voice faded and her face took on an ashen pallor as the reaction to killing a man set in. Then she lost all thoughts of herself. "Archie's been hit."

She turned to see to him, and as she did Rusty appeared from around the side of the wagon, walking on wobbly legs that seemed not to function properly. "Mary Lou ... I think I..." Nate saw a flower of red spreading upon her chest as she fell to the hard earth, her breathing suddenly ragged. Mary Lou ran to her friend, resting her head in her lap. "I think I caught one..." Rusty continued. "But hey, Mary Lou, we sure showed 'em, didn't we?" She rasped.

"Don't talk, Rusty. Save it. We'll get the bullet out and get you to town to a doctor." Mary Lou cradled her, refusing to believe her friend was dying but somehow knowing it was too late.

"Buy yourself a fine dress, girl, you hear me and get one for ... one for me." Rusty sighed and was gone, her chest still, sodden with deep red arterial blood.

"Nooo!" Mary Lou wailed, "no, you can't go, Rusty gal." She hugged her friend and rocked back and forward with Rusty's body cradled in her arms, tears streaming down her face.

Nate cursed out loud. "I should have seen it, I should have put more men on the wagon." He stooped to put an arm around Mary Lou as Rusty's father staggered up, blood dripping from a shoulder wound as his shirt became soaked in it.

"Rusty. My baby girl, dead, gone." His coarse voice was almost a whisper. "Did you have to start shooting?" He gave Nate a look that he would remember until the day he died, soulful and heartbroken. McAllister bent to brush his daughter's hair with his good hand, tears dropping down upon her face, a face that would never again feel the warmth of the morning sun.

Nate turned away, unable to face the scene before him. He stepped into the stirrup and rode back to the scene of the battle. There before him he saw more carnage now that the smoke had cleared. Two of the trail crew were dead and three were wounded. Jake stood over a man, his face ashen, having just thrown up. His hands were shaking, looking at the gun he was holding. "I never knew it would be like that. He just blew up in front of me."

"Just remember, boy, it was you or him." Nate put a comforting hand upon his shoulder. "If you'd let him you'd be lying there dead while they stole your cattle and money." The ground was strewn with the bodies of the outlaws. At least ten had perished, and the others had galloped away as soon as the advantage was lost.

Rory was ejecting the spent cartridges from his Colt, and he looked up. He shook his head. "Man, I thought we were lost back there when Brannigan went for his gun, I was still reaching when you shot him. You called it right, and I've never seen shooting like it. You hit him and..." He looked down at Brannigan's prostrate form. "Wait. Twice, you got him twice before the other two. Damn it, man, who are you? I'm surely glad you're on our side."

Two or three of the others looked on. Some had been in the war and had seen this sort of carnage before, others were new to it and went to throw up, ashamed of their reaction to sudden death.

Nate wondered once again if the killing was getting too easy. Was he now taking this as the easy way out, shoot first and ask questions later?

"How are the girls?" Jim asked concerned for his daughter.

"Mary Lou is fine. Shaken. She killed one and saved my life as I rode up. But Rusty's dead," he said quietly.

"Dead? No, she can't be," Jim cried in anguish.

"Caught a stray bullet aimed at her father, I guess. He's with her now, he took one in the shoulder."

There was stunned silence in the group.

"We'll bury our dead. I'll get a shovel." Then as Jason came up Nate said: "Jas, keep a look out. They might come back, and I don't want to be caught flat footed again."

Jas nodded. "Nate, you did the right thing, without you we'd all be lying dead here now," he finished quietly. "Well done, you brought us through."

"Except poor Rusty."

The scout nodded. "Warn't your fault. No one asked them owl hoots to raid us—and think what they'd have done to them gals happen they'd killed us. Think on that." Then he mounted and went to check if any had remained.

Nate looked around at the devastation before him. "Them or us," he muttered to himself as if to justify his actions in his own mind. *Am I getting gun hungry?* he asked himself. Was it getting easier just to pull a gun with blinding speed and solve the issue that way? *Did you have to start shooting?* Archie McAllister's words echoed through his head.

He didn't know the answer to that, but he decided that he was glad to be alive and relatively unscathed.

Chapter Twenty-Three

They buried Rusty and the others who had died in the gunfight on a knoll above the river a hundred yards or so from where she was shot. The sun would hit it first thing in the morning, silhouetting the crosses against the sky. Mary Lou had carved a hasty cross for Rusty, and Nate read from the Bible over the graves. Everyone who stood there had tears rolling down their cheeks.

After the brief service when the others had gone, Mary Lou stood shaking with grief. McAllister turned and went to her. "It was my fault," she lamented. "She wouldn't have been on the drive if I had encouraged her." Mary Lou moaned between sobs.

"Now you stop that." McAllister cut in harshly. "She was her own woman and knew her own mind. She wouldn't trade the short time she had on this Earth for anythin' different, I'm sure of that. This land is hard, and it breeds hard folks, but good ones, too. She had a good time with you on the drive, probably some of the best days of her life, and I watched her grow and become a woman. Now do as she said, you hear me? Buy that dress, wear it for her and dance at the hoedown."

Mary Lou nodded, her face streaked with tears, and with McAllister's arm around her, the pair walked away from the grave. Mary Lou stood tall as she stopped by the chuck wagon, and Saul looked down at her from the seat of the bedroll wagon. His broken leg was causing him less pain now and he managed the ribbons well enough.

"Y'all right, miss Mary Lou?" he called down to her.

"I will be in time, Saul," she replied with resolve. "Come on, let's get these here wagons into Dodge."

With that she climbed up to the bench seat and picked up the ribbons, kicking off the brake. "Come on there, girls, get up!" she shouted and with more spirit than she thought she could muster, she pushed the mules into action.

Nate looked on, pleased yet sad for her. "Right boys, we're nearly there, Dodge is over that way, let's get this herd rolling!" And for the last time the cowboys hazed the cattle, shouting at them to move. The herd lumbered forward, bellowing and mooing, swinging their huge racks of horns and tossing their heads. It was a fine spring morning and without the previous night's fight it would have been a memorable moment in everyone's mind.

As the day wore on they saw riders pushing up dust and heading in their direction. Everyone tensed for a moment, then seeing only three men through his glass, Nate relaxed. "It's okay. I know one of them, it'll be fine. Keep pushing the herd, we must nearly be there."

Jas cantered in, pulling to a halt. "She's just over there,

Nate, you did it! We'll be in Dodge tonight." He whooped. Everyone's spirits rose, knowing that the end was in sight.

The party of three men got closer, and Nate made out Paul Tranter riding with a stiffer cavalry seat while the two men by his side were clearly cowhands. They got closer and Tranter took off his hat to wave in salute and Nate reciprocated and set off to meet them, with Jim and McBain at his side. They met several yards in front of the herd.

"Nate Carlton, you young devil. How do you do?" Tranter called out. "Why man, it's good to see you. They were giving good odds that you'd never make it," he said.

"What? What do you mean?" Nate recovered from having his hand pumped by the cattle buyer.

"When I received your wire I was excited. The cattle pens were just being put up and I told them they'd need to be ready. They said you'd never do it. When word spread of you taking down Brian Wallace and facing down Old Man Randall and the DR Connected, no one believed it. Then you took on a new herd as a greenhorn and were cutting a virtually unknown trail against Indians and Brannigan's gang—why, I took some good odds on you. Then news came in yesterday from one of the outlaws who was nearly dead and lost his arm. The doc's been busy; two more since. Damn if the odds didn't shorten, so I made some good money on you, my boy, I surely did. And the town's a better place without Brannigan in it.

"You're famous, boy. I'm sorry to say that news of your run in with the boys at Greenville traveled, too! But you're not out of the woods yet. I hear Randall is fuming mad and he's boasting that he'll see you in Hell for what you did to him."

"Damn, I had no idea," Nate said sadly. "I really didn't want that reputation. You still want to buy the cattle?" he asked, hoping to change the subject as the two men with Tranter looked at him with interest.

"I certainly do. Yours is the first herd up here this season, and I'll pay best prices for your beef. How many head do you have?"

Five hundred, give or take. Might even be up to five twenty, we picked up as many as we ate," Nate replied.

"Good, good. This is Chas and Tim. They'll guide your herd into the pens. We'll do a head count as we go through the chute. One of your men can oversee it, and you can get yourself a whisky while we draw up a contract."

"I'll stay with the herd until the job's done, Paul, if that's all right with you. I owe it to the men and the ones we lost, but then I'll happily join you."

"I understand. Well, I'll see you in the Longhorn Saloon and Steak House. They do a fine steak there and you can get a bath!"

They saw the mighty Arkansas River as the town came into sight, with a wide bridge leading straight across it into the town. As they got closer they saw two-and three-story buildings under construction, giving an indication of how mighty the town would become. At this point the main street was called Front Street, and it ran east to west, bisecting the town. Fort Dodge lay just outside the town, recently built with its wooden palisades reflecting sunlight off the newly stripped timber.

The herd was driven into Front Street and aided by two cowhands who pushed it toward the thinning chute and counted. In the end it came to five hundred and twenty-three head, ten with Nate's brand on them.

Smiling to himself he walked away with the stiff, rolling gait of a horseman who had spent many hours in the saddle. He headed along Front Street for the Longhorn Saloon and a date with a bath, a change of clothes and a steak in that order. An hour later he was sitting at a table with Paul Tranter, his steak half eaten, a bottle of red wine and a signed contract between them. A lawyer was also present to oversee things, and they finally drank each other's health.

"Well, sir, you did it! My heartfelt congratulations. Not that I had any doubt from the moment we met back in Brad Dexter's eating house in what seems like many moons ago."

"Well, thank you. It's been quite a turn of events that I could never have foreseen."

"So what are your plans? What will you do now? I'd be happy to back you for another drive, and maybe we could buy a ranch and set up somewhere. The west needs people like us. They're hungry for beef, we can get as much cattle as they want, fatten 'em and bring 'em to market. What do you say?"

"It is an excellent offer, Paul, but I don't know if I'm ready quite yet. One thing the drive taught me if nothing else is that there is a lot of country to see, and I'd like to see some more of it."

"Well, maybe one more drive then. Go down to Texas again, round up some beef, take a crew with you and bring 'em back up. I'll split the profits with you as well as the wages. You've built quite a reputation for yourself. You'll have no trouble getting punchers now. You're the man who took his first drive, blazed a trail, fought injuns and beat Brannigan. Quite a story."

"I'll surely think about it. It does sound tempting. Maybe I could persuade some of the boys from the DR Connected to join me."

"Good, good. Now tonight, what are you planning?"

"Well there is a hoedown planned with some of the ladies from the town, so Mary Lou can go as the saloons are out of bounds to her. They have a church hall and we're inviting the townsfolk along as a sort of celebration. Would you care to join us?"

"I might call in later, I haven't danced in a coon's age. Talking of which, do you remember that beautiful girl Miss Caz Prideaux who sang when we first met in the Texas Lady saloon?" Nate nodded recalling her and the connection they'd made. She was all woman, he remembered, and they had a lot in common.

"Well, I heard a rumor that she was moving up west, maybe Texas. You may well find her in one of the bigger towns if you travel south again," Tranter said, dangling a carrot in front of him.

Nate admitted to himself that his interest was piqued. He often thought of the enigmatic figure and how he would like to reacquaint himself with her, despite her obnoxious manager, who seemed to hold thrall over Caz.

"I'll bear it in mind," he said causally. "Now if you'll excuse me I have a dance to get to." They shook hands and Nate rose and made to leave.

"We'll speak tomorrow, I'm sure, and I'll have the banker's draft for you then. See you here for breakfast."

Nate tipped his hat and strode out a happy man.

By the time Nate got there, the church hall was already alive with people and music. Bright lights illuminated the building and the townsfolk had set up a table as an impromptu bar. The ladies wore their best dresses, and it was a grand affair, as many of the men from the drive were married and not given to hooraying the town. There was a waltz in progress and Nate saw lots of smiling faces amongst the young girls present. Even Saul was happy, tapping his good leg, the other still in a splint as he hobbled with a stick, looking for girls to impress with his tales of the trail.

Then Nate smelled fresh perfume upon the air. "Mister, you owe me a dance," called a voice behind him. He turned to see a smiling girl in a bright pink dress, and it took him a second or two to realize it was Mary Lou. She looked elegant, with newly cut hair all washed and shiny, and she was wearing eye makeup and red lipstick. She was very pretty, he thought to himself, very pretty indeed.

"Ma'am, do I know you? I knew a girl once who was about your height, but she smelled of mule and always wore pants, so it couldn't have been you." He laughed.

"Mister," Mary Lou scowled fiercely, "if'n you don't want to be walking with a stick like Saul over there you'd best learn some manners and dance with me."

Nate bowed, took her in his arms and started to dance around the room. He was an accomplished dancer, light on his feet and a strong leader, having been coached by his mother.

"Why Mister Carlton, you never cease to amaze me. You are graceful, I do declare you'll make up for all my crushed toes," she flirted.

She had grown up on the drive, having seen more of life, and although still grieving for her friend she had taken hold of herself and decided that this was what Rusty would have wanted, so she threw herself into the celebrations. The dance stopped and they went for some punch, then wandered into the evening air onto the porch under the lights of the hall. "Well, Nate you did it. You got us here and you, sir, are a trail boss." She raised her glass to him.

"Why thank you, ma'am," he responded gently. "It was a good drive despite everything, and we all pulled together."

"You maybe don't know what it means to us, all of us. We've got our cattle to market, money for all our new stock and such. It will make a big difference to all the families in our valley, and it's rich land, with lots of potential to grow and make something of it.

"So..." She hesitated slightly. "Do you plan on coming back along our way?"

"I don't know, Mary Lou, maybe I will with a new herd. Tranter has made me an offer. If I take him up on it I'll certainly call in and see you," he finished steadily without trying to encourage her.

She placed her glass on the porch rail. "Nate, it wouldn't work between us, would it?" she offered diffidently.

"Mary Lou, you're lovely and you're quite a girl, but I'm not ready to settle down. I've got country to see and places to go. I'm not right for anybody at the moment."

She nodded, looking up at him with her bright blue eyes shining. "Then will you do something for me?"

"Of course, anything," Nate offered.

"You've ... well, you've been around, seen something of the world. You're not just a green boy from the valley. I ... I want to be kissed the way a woman should be kissed, so I'll know again when I get the same feeling ... But if you don't want to, then I'll understand." She dropped her eyes, fearing his rejection.

Nate smiled down at her, lifting her chin with his fore-finger. He started to kiss her gently then took her in a crushing embrace and deepened it into a passionate kiss that seemed to last for eternity to the girl. He released her gently and held her at arm's length, her chest heaving, her breathing heavy and her face flushed. "Now I'd better go before you change my mind," he said. "Good night, Mary Lou." He smiled down at her gently, pecked her on the cheek and walked off into the darkness.

Chapter Twenty-Four

The morning sun streamed through the windows of Nate's room, with the drapes offering little shade as he had slept with the window open, and the breeze had pushed them apart. He scratched his head and yawned. Free of living on the edge for weeks on end he had slept deeply for twelve solid hours, barely moving. He got up, stretched and splashed water from the jug into the bowl to wash. Pushing aside the drapes he saw the town was already alive. He washed and dressed, slinging his gun belt around his waist, ordered tea, and went out to the barber's shop for a shave.

There he was disturbed by Mary Lou. "Nate, oh, Nate! I'm glad I've found you," she said. "There are men in town looking for you and one of them is threatening to kill you."

The barber wiped the final suds from Nate's face with a hot towel and removed the sheet from his waist to expose the Colt Police Special he had tucked in his waist band. Mary Lou looked down at it.

"Oh no, Nate, not another gun battle. Can't you just ride away?"

"Now, Mary Lou, just calm down and tell me everything," he said gently. "No one's going to kill anyone."

"He is. It's Mr. Randall, I recognise him from back at the house. He has five men with him and they all look mean."

He urged her to tell him everything, and when she finished she asked: "What are you going to do?"

"First, I'm going to see the sheriff. I'll avoid trouble if I can, but if not, I'll face it. I'm not running away."

Nate settled the Colt in his left holster and slung his gun belt on again, tying down the cord around his leg and slipping off the thong around the hammer. Settling the belt, he put his hat on, paid the nervous looking barber and walked into the street, heading for the sheriff's office. He had met Charlie Bassett the evening before, and they'd exchanged a few words. He had liked the man's stamp and got on well with him as he seemed a good solid lawman.

He knocked and went into the sheriff's office. "Morning, sheriff," he greeted.

"Morning Nate, you sober?" Bassett grinned amiably. He was a medium sized man who wore a derby hat over curly brown hair. He had a slight paunch and was well set up. But he wore a gun like he knew how to use it and had shrewd, all-seeing eyes that sized a man up pretty quickly.

"I left early. I was dog tired, and it was time. Hate to get drunk anyway and lose control. And talking of losing control, I hear that there are some men looking for me with one of 'em threatening to kill me. From what I'm told, I suspect it's David Randall of the DR Connected. Now we had a bit of a ruckus on the trail, and it looks like he is trying to finish it."

"Let me hear it all," Bassett said.

When Nate finished his story, the sheriff considered all he had been told.

"Well now it's like this. There ain't nothing I can do until Randall—if it is him—makes a move. What happens on the trail is well outside my jurisdiction. But, if he cuts up rough in my town then I'll butt in. I can't help you any more than that."

"That's fine, sheriff, all I wanted to do is let you know the score. I won't go looking for trouble and I'll be out of town in two or three days anyway. But he owes me money to the tune of a hundred head of cattle, and I can handle all he's got to give."

"You might find yourself playin' against a stacked deck," the sheriff warned.

"Well, if it is, I've got twelve cards to call," Nate said, patting his guns. "But I will try to avoid gun play at all costs. I just wanted you to know."

"Fair enough, I'll be watching," Bassett said.

"Good enough. Now I'm off to the Longhorn to meet Paul Tranter. I'll be seeing you, sheriff." Nate tipped his hat and was gone. He walked up the street, warily, looking left and right, hands never straying far from his gun butts. He made it to the Longhorn Saloon and stepped inside the swinging doors, moving quickly to the left letting his eyes adjust to the light and assessing the room. All seemed peaceful, and Randall was not present.

He spotted Paul Tranter and walked over to his table just as he was finishing breakfast.

"Morning, Nate," he said cheerfully, wiping his mouth with his napkin. "You're an early riser." He looked spry and well dressed as ever, sporting a fancy embroidered vest and favoring a planter's hat over a Stetson.

"Morning, Paul. Yes, I slept well and hit the sack early. Seems like I might need to stay alert."

"I heard that there was trouble brewing. What will you do?"

"Face it like I always do. If it is Randall then he owes me just over fifteen hundred dollars for ninety-five head of cattle. A tidy sum, and I won't let him get away without paying it."

"Well, it looks like you're going to get your chance, because here he comes now," Tranter warned Nate, raising his eyebrows toward the door.

Nate turned slightly, keeping his back to the wall, and there was Randall, flanked by Ted Lineman, Steve Jones and Joe Brock, both from the incident outside Jim's house in the valley, where they nearly hanged him.

"Paul, this will be gun trouble, but I'll try to avoid it if I can. Get yourself out of the line of fire, I don't want you mixed up in my troubles," he muttered quietly.

Tranter ignored him, stayed seated and watched the panoply play out before him. With the ingrained knowledge of such matters the western crowd moved away from the impeding action, leaving a clear path for Randall to get to Nate's table.

Randall looked bigger and more formidable than ever.

He had lost a bit of his paunch on the trail and looked mean and ready for anything. His heavy eyes missing nothing. The other three men fanned out in his wake, eyes ready for trouble, hands close to their gun butts. Randall stopped about twenty feet away.

"Get up, Carlton. Nobody holds me at gunpoint and lives to talk about it. You're a two bit brush popper, and today will be the last time you hold a gun on any man."

Nate looked up as though he was only just aware of the newcomer. He responded in a mild, mocking voice. "Oh, it's you, Randall. Have you come to bring me my money for the ninety five head you took, in accordance with your rules? I calculate that you owe me fifteen hundred and twenty dollars. Or are you the type of man who is going to welch on the deal? I guess you might be, given the attempted murder of an innocent homesteader who you, along with your two bully boys, were going to hang for holding three head of cattle that I offered to buy in return for his life. But no, you wanted to see him hang in front of his family for his honest mistake. You're an evil bully, Randall. But the man still lives, thank God. He's here now and we took his herd along with a few others to market." Nate continued riding the man, getting him angry, for he knew that an angry man is slower and more prone to making stupid mistakes.

"Get up and I'll make you eat those words with your dying breath. But I won't shoot a man sitting down."

"That's good to know. Do those morals of yours include your gunny friends? Are they going to take the pot four to one? I thought better of you, Ted." Nate nodded at Lineman.

"They'll stay out of it. It's just you and me. Now get up and draw."

The atmosphere in the saloon was at breaking point, the tension palpable. Nate remained calm as he replied.

"The thing is, Randall, you're just not good enough and I don't trust those sidewinders at your back not to gun me down the second I stand. So—"

And with a flash of movement his right hand appeared from where it had been resting on his lap, with his Colt Police Special lined, cocked, and aimed at Randall's large belly. Seeing the blur of movement, Randall made his play. He had been watching Nate, but looking at the wrong gun. He thought that he would draw from his right holster. But he was not in the same class as Nate and would have died if Nate had squeezed the trigger. There were gasps around the room at the sight of the gun appearing as if by magic, and Randall stood transfixed, expecting at any moment to breathe his last.

"See? If I was as ruthless as you, you'd be dead now. But here's what we're going to do. You boys, you too Ted, drop your guns or your boss gets it. You and me, Randall, we'll settle it another way. Go on, drop your belts," Nate ordered, his voice harsher now.

Then a voice from behind finished the arguments: the doors opened permitting Jim and others of the trail crew to enter all armed with long guns. "You tried to hang me, Randall," Jim said, "and now the boot's on the other foot, so do as he says."

The DR Connected men dropped their gun belts while Randall stood motionless, his face suffused with rage.

Nate stood, pinwheeled the Colt and placed it back in its holster. "Now Randall," he continued, "you reckon you're the old bull of the woods and can lick any man with your fists. That's your boast, if I recall it. Well, I'm going to beat you for the bully you are. You're nothing but a big man with a crew at your back, you two-faced welcher," Nate goaded, unbuckling his belt and dropping it on the table.

Randall grinned evilly and started to unbuckle his gun belt, striding forward with an angry look on his face. When he got closer he lashed out with the gun belt, whipping Nate across the face. It was an unexpected move and caught the younger man by surprise. He then ran in with his fists, smashing a left to Nate's ribs and a right that caught partly on Nate's upraised hand, a reflex at being lashed in the face. Nate was driven backwards over the table, and it was this that saved him from being stomped by Randall's boots. He went with the roll, carrying on aware of the pain in his side. Pushing the table aside Randall moved in, fists and feet ready.

Nate swiveled around, swinging his right leg just as Randall went to stomp him. Caught with one leg raised, Randall went down hard, hitting the wooden floor with a thump. Winded and bruised, Nate was in no state to capitalize on it and did not want to wrestle with him, as he would be giving away at least twenty pounds. He staggered upright, breathing heavily, his ribs hurting with every breath.

"Come on, Randall, let's see how you are without a gun belt as a whip."

With a bull-like roar the older man lurched to his feet and closed in, his hands moving like a boxer. Somewhere,

Nate thought, he had been taught some science, not just muscle. Nate dropped his guard and Randall threw an overarm right. Nate ducked it, raising his left shoulder and forearm and twisting his hips, slamming a right straight to Randall's ribs. He went to smash a jab to the jaw but Randall was game and didn't fold. He got his guard up, protected his jaw and threw two straight jabs at Nate's head. One landed and he saw stars, the other caught his guard, which was driven back into his nose by the sheer force of the blow.

Partially blinded with tears Nate advanced swinging, keen to land a hit and gain himself time to clear his sight and get set. The wild swings barely registered against Randall's bulk and strength. He closed and enveloped Nate's slighter frame in a bear hug, his massive strength crushing Nate's already bruised ribs in a painful embrace. Much longer and Nate realized he would pass out. With his arms pinioned Nate went for any advantage, but realized that Randall with his rough house experience had dropped his chin to give him no chance of a Liverpool kiss. Yet it left one option. Nate extended his neck, secured Randall's ear between his teeth and bit down hard. Randall gave an involuntary howl, raising his huge shaggy head up and bringing a hand to his damaged ear. Nate didn't hesitate. He dropped his forehead straight onto the now exposed bridge of Randall's nose, then drove the palm of his now freed right hand straight under his chin, driving the head back before smashing his knee up between Randall's legs.

The knee didn't do as much damage as he would have wished, but it gave Nate a breather. He stepped back and took a new stance, hands out and balanced, that seemed strange to western eyes.

Randall roared: "I'm going to rip you apart!" Yet he came in wary, knowing the quality of the man he faced, who was more than just a kid with a gun as he'd supposed. He feinted with a left and went to throw a right, driving from the hip with his full body weight behind it.

Nate had waited, seemingly exposed with arms down, out and balanced. As the right came in, he pivoted on the left foot, swinging up in a fast roundhouse kick that seemed to come from nowhere. Randall wasn't expecting it and he saw it way too late. The toe of Nate's boot caught him right on the temple and he dropped like a stone upon impact. Nate thought he had killed him. Everyone just stood there, amazed.

Through heaving breaths Nate said: "See if he's still alive."

Ted moved forward to kneel by his side. "He is, but he's breathing hard. Someone get a doctor," he ordered. "Never thought I'd see the day. You're one hell of a fighter, Nate, with guns or fists. But I thought he had you there once or twice."

"So did I, Ted, so did I." Nate sighed, holding his ribs. "When he wakes up, tell him I'm still coming for the banker's draft for my cattle."

"You just don't give up, do you, boy?"

"No," Nate said and staggered towards Paul Tranter's table.

"Hell of a fight, here have a cup of coffee." Tranter poured a cup and handed it to Nate. "Don't worry, I'll see you get that draft. If he argues I'll destroy his reputation for good."

Just then Sheriff Bassett walked in. "Looks like you got it sorted then, Nate. Obliged for not shooting him, it would have made life difficult." He tipped his hat at Nate. "All right, folks, show's over, no more trouble from anyone." Here he looked sternly at the three DR Connected hands.

The tough puncher, Bob, who was considered very gun handy, muttered: "That's the second time you've made me surrender my guns, Carlton. One day we'll have a reckoning, just you see if we don't."

Nate ignored him and sipped the coffee. "Well, Paul, I guess that decides it, I think I've worn out my welcome here for the time being. I'll take you up on your offer. I'll go down to Texas and put another herd together."

Afterword

A message from Simon:

I know that you have a million choices of books to read and I can't tell you how much it means to me that you chose time to read one of my books. I really hope that you enjoyed it and found it entertaining.

If you did I would appreciate a few more minutes of your time, if I may humbly ask you to leave a review for other readers who may be trying to select their next reading material.

If for any reason you were not satisfied with this book please do let me know by emailing me at simon@ simonfairfaxauthor.com

The satisfaction of my readers and feedback are important to me.

About the Author

ABOUT THE AUTHOR

Simon Fairfax writes in three different genres: International financial thrillers, medieval fiction and Westerns.

He is a former Chartered Surveyor, Editor of an online polo magazine (having played polo for a number of years) and has practiced martial arts, fencing and shooting. He now restores old classic sports cars for fun.

As a lover of crime thrillers and espionage, Simon turned what is seen by others as a dull 9 – 5 job into something that is exciting, and as close to real life as possible, with Rupert Brett, his unwilling hero.

His latest medieval series now has five books released in a proposed 6 book series. The first, A Knight and a Spy 1410, is set in a tumultuous time at the English court. It tells the story of Jamie de Grispere, squire in training and his two companions as they fight the French to save Calais, Welsh treason and Scottish revolts. The last in the series, A Knight and a Spy 1415 will be published in February 2024.

Details of all his books can be found at www.simonfairfax.com or email him at simonfairfaxauthor@gmail.com